Can't Catch Me, I'm the Gingerbread Man

The band had stopped during the speech, but it started back suddenly with a fanfare, a call to arms. All the contestants at my table grabbed their aprons and rushed to get in line for what the speaker called "The Grand March." I grabbed my apron, too, gave Mom a hug, and ran after them, putting it on as I went. If he'd seen me, Coach Kenepker would have kicked me off the hockey team and Lenny would have died laughing.

Also by Jamie Gilson

Dial Leroi Rupert, DJ

Do Bananas Chew Gum?

Double Dog Dare

4B Goes Wild

Harvey, the Beer Can King

Hello, My Name Is Scrambled Eggs

Hobie Hanson, Greatest Hero of the Mall

Hobie Hanson, You're Weird

Soccer Circus

Sticks and Stones and Skeleton Bones

Thirteen Ways to Sink a Sub

Wagon Train 911

Can't Catch Me, I'm the Gingerbread Man

Jamie Gilson

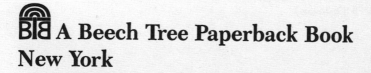 A Beech Tree Paperback Book
New York

Excerpt from "Ugly Chile" by Clarence Williams,
copyright MCMXVII, MCMXLVI, renewed by
Shapiro, Bernstein & Co., Inc., has been used by
permission.

The Library of Congress has cataloged the Lothrop,
Lee & Shepard Books edition of *Can't Catch Me, I'm
the Gingerbread Man* as follows:
Gilson, Jamie.
Can't catch me, I'm the gingerbread man.
SUMMARY: When the family health food store burns
down, 12-year-old Mitch is even more determined to
win first prize in a Bakeathon with his special
gingerbread.
ISBN 0-688-00435-0—ISBN 0-688-00436-9 (lib. bdg.)
[1. Contests—Fiction. 2. Baking—Fiction.
3. Family life—Fiction] I. Title.
PZ7.G4385Can [Fic] 80-39748

10 9 8 7 6 5 4 3 2 1
First Beech Tree Edition, 1997
ISBN 0-688-15488-3

For my mother,
Sally Chisam

Contents

Can't Catch Me, I'm the Gingerbread Man

1

It's the Gary Conrad Show

GLORIA STUCK HER HEAD IN THE DOOR OF THE GREEN-room of Studio A where I was sitting, gnawing on my fingernails. "Hey, Mitch, you watching the show?" she asked me. "It's great tonight! Dawn Couture is fabulous. Lousy actress, but she tells incredible stories. Does it without a writer, too. Hold on fifteen more minutes, baby, and Gary will be ready for you."

I smiled automatically and tried to press my cowlick down with a damp palm. "Thanks . . . Gloria. . . ." My voice was so squeaky I didn't recognize it. Gloria was all of her name I knew. She was in charge of guests waiting to be on the Gary Conrad Show. It's on at eight o'clock every weeknight, coast to coast. I was going to be Gary Conrad's guest. Me, Mitch McDandel. They'd flown me all the way from Chicago to Los Angeles.

The sound on the TV monitor was turned down, but I could see Gary and Dawn Couture throw their heads back and laugh. I'd never seen her in a movie. She was always R-rated.

"I'm scared," I told Gloria.

"Oh, no need for that." She brushed that thought away with a flick of her purple fingernails. "They're a marvelous audience. They'll absolutely eat you up." Gloria looked like she was a movie star, too, though when I'd asked her if she was, she'd giggled. Her voice was warm and sqwooshy. She had a wide layer of black eyelashes and her face sparkled like it had tiny flecks of gold on it.

"Walt Milliken goes on in about two minutes," she told me. "He and Gary are going to shoot baskets before they talk. You know who he is?"

"Everybody knows Walt Milliken," I said. "He's the best basketball player in the world."

"Have you met Alexandra?" she went on, motioning to the woman with dark hair who sat huddled in a leather chair, reading. Alexandra glanced up. Next to the gray leather chair were two large boxes with air holes in them. "Alexandra is our zoo person. She'll bring in some fantastic animals later on so Gary can play with them. Something cute like a cobra and a mongoose. Alexandra, this is Mitch McDandel. He's from . . ." She looked at me blankly. Alexandra sighed and closed her book.

"Evanston, Illinois," I told her.

"Right, right. And he's . . . how old?" Gloria asked.

"Twelve, going on thirteen," I told her.

"Going on thirteen. That's precious. He's going on thirteen. And he's on the show because of some cooking thing. He looks perfect, don't you think? Red hair, freckles. All he needs is a missing front tooth. Anyway, Gary thought Mitch would be fabulous for a little human interest. Something to play off against all the glitter. You know, Boy Cook." She flashed her huge smile and swept out of the room.

Alexandra started back with her book again. Then she turned it over in her lap and said something to one of the cage-boxes beside her. From inside I heard small scratches and gurgles. I wondered if the animals were as scared as I was. I was biting my fingernails, again. The more I thought of me being on *the* Gary Conrad Show the more incredible it seemed, and the more I could feel my heart beat faster.

I kept thinking over the last few days, remembering how this had all happened. I decided it began just five days before, the day of the hockey game. Everything was probably all set up before then, like a hockey puck sitting on the ice waiting to be slapped, but it wasn't until that Thursday that I saw it fly.

2

Outlook Bright Today

WE RAN LIKE CRAZY DOWN SHERMAN STREET, LENNY, Aaron, and me. Whenever we missed the school bus and had to walk home, we always raced that block before stopping to eat at my parents' health food store, Sunshine. Even in winter it was a good race-track—the snow was shoveled early and the sidewalk was so wide that anybody who saw us coming could dodge without falling into the street.

I gave it all I had. My horoscope that morning had said, "Outlook bright today. Go for what you want and you'll get it." Mom always read my horoscope at breakfast after she'd read us hers and Dad's. I remembered mine all day. Dad, who didn't believe the sky told anything but weather, always laughed at his.

Thursday's horoscope was true so far, though. I'd aced a math test that three guys had flunked flat. As I ran, the ice cold January air stung my lungs, and halfway down the block I yelled, "Can't catch me, I'm the gingerbread man."

I knew I shouldn't have said it. Aaron, who's five inches shorter than I am, sailed past me, and by the time we reached the new supermarket near the corner of Main and Sherman, Lenny and I were both eating dust.

"Gingerbread man, you are catchable," Aaron said as he leaned against the lamppost, waiting. He wasn't even out of breath. "When that crazy cooking contest is over maybe you can get in shape again for hockey. The only game we lost, we lost when you turned cook and made the finals of that crazy contest."

Actually, I hadn't just turned cook. I'd taken all the cooking classes Mom had given at Sunshine so I knew a lot about natural food and how to fix it, not just bragging either. My whole-wheat lasagna with spinach is practically legendary. I make Caesar's salad with sprouts for people who don't dream it's health food. My ratatouille is excellent, served hot in winter or cold in summer. But it's my gingerbread that made me famous. I'd entered it in the ABC Bakeathon, a big national baking contest. When they'd called three weeks earlier to tell me I'd made the Bakeathon finals, I'd yelped like a coyote. I could have taken off straight into the sky. My horoscope that day had said, "Make plans to gain your finest goals," and boy, did I make plans—a ten-speed bike, a tiny calculator that does *everything*, a noodle maker so I could make tomato linguini. I figured if I won money I could spend it.

Now the contest was only two days away, and I knew I was going to win. It was hard to think about hockey or anything else. I was going to *win*.

"It's OK, McGingerbread. I'll come to your big game tonight and cheer like a madman. If that doesn't pull you through, nothing will," Lenny told me, as we dodged women with shopping carts. They were coming out of Stop and Save, this huge new supermarket that moved in where the Scandinavian furniture store used to be.

Stop and Save had cut into Sunshine's business pretty bad. The problem was the big store was new and it was cheap and it sold health food as well as regular groceries, and shoe polish, and bleach, and green plants, and sneakers, and delicatessen things that we didn't sell. It was bad news for us.

"But you guys are really going to have to hustle against those Trailblazers," Lenny went on. "My insults may not throw them off totally."

"My horoscope says it's a good day for me," I told them. "It's in the stars."

Lenny laughed like he always did when I told him about my horoscope, and shook his head like I was clearly wacko. "I stopped reading that stuff," he said, "the day it told me my lucky star had just been sucked into a black hole."

"Yeah, but does it say we'll win tonight?" Aaron

interrupted, as we rounded the corner.

"The outlook is bright," I told him.

"Then you better shine, Ace," he said.

Lenny grabbed my arm. "My stomach is a yawning cave. Let's stop first at Corso's. I need a hot dog."

"Those hot dogs," I said, "are the pits." Corso's was the month-old hot dog stand right on the corner next door to Sunshine. "Mom says Corso's hot dogs are packed with disgusting preservatives and additives," I told him. "What's more, they smell up our shop."

"It's perfume," Lenny said, pushing Corso's bright red door open and taking a deep breath. It was the first time I'd been inside. Mom hated the place so much I'd just stayed away, and, like her, I didn't like the hot dog smell. But it was too cold to just hang around outside and wait. The store was painted in red-and-yellow stripes. It didn't *look* so bad. Over the counter a huge red-and-brown neon hot dog sprinkled with green neon relish flashed off and on. Behind the counter a high school kid was dipping batches of fries in and out of sputtering hot fat, trying to keep up with orders. There was such a crowd of kids that the heat of them and their coats was steaming up the front window. I grabbed a free table littered with stacks of plastic hot dog baskets, and waited for Lenny and Aaron to order at the counter. That stuff is just junk food. I leave it alone. At the next table, a girl fooling around with a mustard holder squeezed it so hard a great gob shot in the air like a volcano erupting yellow.

"Cut that out," Mr. Corso yelled at her from the cash register. Then he spotted me and laughed. "Hey, McDandel, your mother know you're in here? Naughty, naughty."

"I'm not eating," I explained. Last time I saw him, he and Mom were shouting at each other about his exhaust vents. She'd also mentioned to him how crummy and unnatural his menu was.

"You're not eating, then you're not sitting," he said. "Got lots of people in here who need chairs." But just then Aaron brought his mound of fries to the table and started squirting them with catsup, and Lenny showed up with two hot dogs and a Pepsi, so Corso didn't throw me out. He just rang up somebody else's order.

Three girls from school were hovering behind us, so we let them put their stuff on our table.

"Hey, Lenny, I bet you didn't know that Karen likes you. Do you like her?" one of the girls asked him.

"Crazy about her." He took a huge bite of hot dog and sighed with happiness as he chewed. Then he gulped down some Pepsi, wiped his mouth with a napkin, and went on. "In fact, I'm thinking about asking her to elope this Saturday."

"Barbara likes you, too," another one told him.

"Does she know I'm writing a symphony for her?" he asked. "She's so noteworthy."

Mr. Corso was clearing off the table next to us. "Hey, kid," he said to me. "Congratulations. I read in the paper about your cooking contest. Big money. You gonna win?"

"Sure am," I told him. "It's good gingerbread. I'm going to win first prize."

"I tell you what," he went on, saying it low like it was a big secret between us, "if you win, you make a few pans of that stuff up for me every day and I'll sell it to the kids here after school. Gingerbread's good on a cold day. What d'you say? These guys are bottomless pits." He stared around the room at all the disappearing hot dogs and french fries. "Make a little dough with a little dough, what d'you say?"

"Thanks," I told him. I mean, it was really nice of him. He and my mom fought a lot, so he didn't need to do that. "Thanks, I don't know if it'd work, but . . ."

He shrugged. "Well, good luck," he said, and walked away.

"So I told my dad," Lenny was telling Aaron and the girls when I tuned in, "that I play good jazz piano because I've got your blues genes. . . ." And we all laughed.

Back at the cash register, Mr. Corso rang up somebody else's order. "McDandel," he called to me, "what do you think of that new sign in your window?" My mom had been making signs lately. For the past month or so she'd put up a new one every couple of days. She liked to draw and it gave her something to do when business was slow.

Someone put a quarter in the jukebox and the place began to pound with music, the red-and-yellow stripes shimmering.

I shook my head. "What's it say?"

"Look for yourself," he shouted over the noise, and turned to talk to the high school girl who worked afternoons as cashier.

"Mr. Corso says my mom has made another sign for the window," I told the group. "The one yesterday said 'Let our ever-lovin' Sun Shine on you.' She's big on signs." I laughed.

"The one today isn't very funny," one of the girls said, drawing a line of catsup down a french fry and then dotting it at the bottom like a punctuation mark. "I saw it when we went past. It says 'Going Out of Business.'" She popped the french fry into her mouth.

"'Going Out of Business'?" I gasped. My heart started beating faster than the music.

"Didn't your folks tell you?" Aaron asked me.

I shook my head, numb.

"My mom used to buy honeycombs there," one of the girls told me.

"Maybe they just decided today," Lenny said, finishing off his first hot dog.

"I don't believe it!" The chair fell over as I grabbed my coat and headed for the door. Lenny and Aaron gathered up what was left of their food and followed after.

The wind blasted us as we ran next door, our coats dragging on the sidewalk.

The sign was there, all right. It wasn't a big sign, but it was hand-lettered in pow orange. And it packed a wallop. Lenny started to laugh. Then Aaron. Then so did I. Mom's sign didn't say "Going Out of Business." It said "Going Out *for* Business." Geeeez.

The bell jingled as we opened the front door. Mom was sitting behind the counter, reading. There were no customers, but we could hear the beat from next door.

"That sign," I told Mom, "almost gave me a heart attack."

She smiled broadly like that was the idea. "Hello, gentlemen. Welcome. Is it so hot suddenly that you were running with your coats off? Glad you like the sign. It's an eyecatcher, isn't it. Sunburst orange. I made it this morning in my free time. It even brought in a few people, but a stampede it wasn't."

Mom handed us a bowl of carob-covered raisins and saw Lenny clutching his spare hot dog. She shook her head at him. "Leonard Barker," she said, pointing to the door, "out, out. You know I can't stand the sight or smell of those hot dogs. And I've already *got* the smell."

Aaron stuck the rest of his french fries in his coat pocket and wiped his mouth with his sleeve.

"But *I* can stand them," Lenny said, "and I'm the one who counts—one, two, three, four—"

"Out," she said, "jokes and all. You can come back in when you're finished and eat something good."

"I've got to practice the piano, anyway," he told her with a shrug. "Me and the dog here will just run on home. See you guys later."

"Pick you up at six-fifteen," Aaron called to him as the door closed.

"Your father's at the bank," Mom said to me. "And there's really no new stock for you to unpack since we've been cutting back. So why don't you two just help yourselves to something." Aaron and I poked around in the refrigerator case for yogurts, and then sat with them on a bench near the cookbooks.

"Tonight's hockey," I reminded her, taking a bite of good creamy lemon yogurt, "so I can't work much past five, anyway." The doorbell clanged and a woman rushed in, out of breath. She wore a heavy plaid muffler, but her cheeks were red with cold. She went dashing up and down the aisles. "I'm in the middle of a cake and I need a pound of confectioners' sugar, some bitter chocolate, and a box of waxed paper," she called from the back of the store. "Where do you keep them?"

"I'm sorry," Mom told her. "Waxed paper we just don't stock. And we don't carry sugar or chocolate. We've some honey, if you like, or molasses. We sell carob, which you can use as a chocolate substitute."

"But I don't want carob or molasses. I want confectioners' sugar and bitter chocolate," the woman said, stalking toward the front. "Aren't you a grocery store?"

"A natural food grocery store," Mom said. "Refined sugar robs your body of B vitamins and chocolate isn't in keeping with a healthy diet, so we don't eat them or sell them to our customers. Waxed paper is a good idea, though. A lot of people are allergic to plastic."

"So what's wrong with chocolate cake? It's my mother's recipe and she lived to be ninety. No, don't tell me," she said, throwing her hands up. "It's just my luck when I'm in a hurry to run into a health food fanatic. No wonder you're going out of business." She flung the muffler over her face and barreled away.

"There's a big new grocery store around the corner," Mom murmured after the door had slammed.

"I think I'd better go now," Aaron said, embarrassed, handing me his half-empty yogurt cup. "My dad will pick you up around six-fifteen for the game."

"Thanks, Aaron, for always taking Mitch," Mom said. "Thank your father for me. I am sorry we can't help with the driving, but the store seems to go on forever." She looked outside and her nose twitched like she smelled something she didn't like.

"See you," Aaron said, and he ducked out the door just as Mr. Corso walked in.

"Well, Mrs. McDandel," Mr. Corso said, standing inside and looking over the empty shop, "you really are something. I mean it, that's some sign you made." He grinned and nodded toward the window. "I thought at first you were going into early retirement."

"I may just do that, Mr. Corso," Mom told him, rubbing her forehead.

"Your son just paid me a nice visit," he said.

"Yes," Mom told him dryly, "I saw evidence of that."

"I only went in with Lenny and Aaron," I said quickly.

"Oh, he didn't *eat* anything, if that's what you're worried about."

"Mr. Corso, is that what you came to tell me, that Mitch was in your dreadful place? You're here as a tattletale?"

Mr. Corso stopped smiling and his voice turned hard. "As a matter of fact, I came about the exterminator."

"Forget the exterminator."

"That's what the mice tell me." He bounced it back to her fast like a Ping-Pong ball.

"We don't bring poison into the store, Mr. Corso. Anything that kills mice will, it follows, harm people." She pointed over to the bulletin board. "I post certificates saying our fresh fruits and vegetables have no pesticides on them. We keep our store neat and tidy so we have no mice."

"I keep *my* store 'neat and tidy' and I *do* have mice. I think they come from this place. Last month when I moved in, I had the exterminator. Last *week* I had the exterminator. Today I saw a mouse. He's your mouse. I know it."

"Maybe you should get a cat, Mr. Corso."

"Maybe you should get an exterminator, Mrs. McDandel."

"No. I've told you before, no, and that's final. Almost ten years now we've maintained this store without an exterminator. We're certainly not going to start poisoning our customers now."

Mr. Corso sighed deeply. "I could wish for a better neighbor."

"So could I. When your place was a dress shop, we got along with the owners just fine. How long do you expect us to keep customers in a store that smells like hot dog heaven and vibrates with that earthquake of sound?"

"*I* do it. Since I moved to this big corner spot, my

business has tripled. Maybe you should try moving to my old place. It's near the university between a bookstore and a camp fitter. Very quiet and almost odorless. Roaches we had there, but no mice."

"Thank you for your advice," Mom said, getting really mad now and moving toward Mr. Corso like she was going to practice her judo on him. "Maybe you should leave."

"Maybe you're right," he said, and the bell jammered when he slammed the door.

Mom folded her arms tight and narrowed her eyes. "That man . . ." Then she gave me a little half-smile. "What ever made you go *in* his store?" she asked.

I shrugged. "Lenny likes his hot dogs. Whatever made you think up that crazy sign?"

She laughed, and started straightening the bottles of vitamins at the check-out counter. Then she pointed to the book she'd been reading as we came in, *How to Write Advertising That Sells*. "My handy-dandy advertising manual tells me I can make an effective slogan just by changing a word or two in an old, familiar saying. It worked." Giving me a swat, she said, "It's almost five. You'd better be off. You've a game to play in that funny yellow-and-black suit that makes you look like a mutant bumblebee."

She always said that. I liked it. Me as a mutant bumblebee.

"If you have time, be sure to bake your gingerbread for school. Didn't you tell Mrs. Archer you'd bring some tomorrow? You all ready to fly through the air like Superman, Saturday?"

"I'm going to pack tomorrow night, but I don't know how ready I am to fly. How about you?"

She shrugged. "The cheering section doesn't need to look sensational. I'll just throw a few things in a bag."

I pulled my Black Hawks cap down over my ears and zipped my coat up high. The sky outside was gray and looked more and more like snow. On the way toward the door I saw the sign in the window again.

"Remember my horoscope this morning?" I asked Mom. " 'Go for what you want and you'll get it?' You know what I want? I want you to take that sign down."

She looked over at the big sheet of paper. "Oh, Mitch, it took such a long time to make. You really think it's not a good idea?"

"You know what everybody *thinks* it says. That's awful. Things aren't that bad, are they?"

"I suppose you're right," she said, not answering my question. "OK, tear it down, if you like. I can't fight a winning horoscope."

The front door jingled open. A man who said he didn't know what he'd do without us ordered a pound each of chick-peas, millet, and barley, and a quart of the peanut butter I'd ground myself. While Mom scooped the grains out of their bins, I climbed into the window, ripped off the orange words, and stuffed them into the trash.

"Onward!" she called as I left for home.

Mr. Corso waved through his steamy window when I passed, and I waved back, without thinking.

Ice like little BB's began to fall with the rain. But everything was all right, I told myself. That crazy sign didn't mean anything. Sunshine wasn't really going out of business. Sales were down, but what could you expect with a giant around the corner. The Jets are going to win tonight, I thought. I'm going to win Saturday. The outlook is sunshine bright. I brushed away the rain that was beading on my face.

"Horoscope," I said out loud, "you just better be right."

3

Fight, Fight, Fight

ZAP! THE PUCK FLEW IN TO SCORE BEFORE I SAW ANY-body put a stick to it.

"McGingerbread!" Using his hands as a megaphone, Lenny leaned over the ledge above the ice rink. "A goalie's supposed to keep the biscuits *out* of the oven," he called, like he was explaining the rules. That was the second time I'd let it slide in to burn us. That made the score Trailblazers 2, Jets 2, as the buzzer sounded for the end of the second period. Somehow, I just couldn't keep my mind on the game. I kept remembering that "Going Out for Business" sign, and wondering why we were keeping our stock so low. Tonight, I thought, I'll make Mom and Dad tell me how bad things really are at the store.

"If you can't take the heat, get out of the kitchen, McGingerbread!" Lenny yelled.

The yellow plastic goalie's mask covered my whole face, so he couldn't tell whether I saw him or not. I turned my head the other way to make him think

I hadn't and skated off toward the coach, old Fight-Fight-Fight Kenepker.

We were playing the Trailblazers in the Park District's Pee Wee League. It was halfway through the season and we'd only lost one.

"Smash 'em, Jets," a kid yelled.

There were maybe thirty people watching us, most of them family, and they were all good yellers.

"You guys stink tonight, you know that?" Coach Kenepker was saying as I skidded up, but then he always said that, even when it was 5–0, our favor. All the yellow masks stared at him. "You're skating like marshmallows. Don't you want to *win*?"

The masks mumbled and tilted down toward the ice.

I want to win, I thought. You know I want to win. It was warm inside the mask and I closed my eyes and saw myself with a three-foot trophy in one hand and a batch of cooking cash in the other. Instead of a bike and a calculator and all those things I didn't really need, I'd turn the cash over to my folks so they could make Sunshine better than any supermarket. When I give it to them, I thought, they'll say no, put it in your savings account for later, and I'll say no, it's a family business and I'm a third of the family. I'll say—

"And what do you say to that, McDandel?" Coach Kenepker barked.

I had no idea what he'd asked me. "I . . . I . . . I've only let two slip by."

"That's two too many. Those twerps have tied us. McDandel, you're supposed to be eyeballing that puck, not dreaming up recipes for wheat germ soup."

A couple of haw-haws echoed behind the masks and Mr. Kenepker grinned, glad they'd gotten his joke. He'd heard about the contest from somebody and he thought it was *very* funny.

"You got to really go out for the kill," the coach went on, turning to Aaron who was standing next to me. "Colby's the real hustler tonight. The rest of you hustle like that and we'll knock the pants off those snot-nosed Trailblazers, beat 'em 8 to 2. Aaron may be a little kid, but he throws that welterweight around. Hockey's a rough game. You got to play it that way or you'll lose."

"Another thing, McDandel. Don't flop so much," the coach continued. "Once you're down, you're down, like . . . like one of your cakes that fell in the oven." All the other masks turned to look at me. In the distance we could hear the other team cheer, but on our side there was a long, soggy silence.

"OK, Jets," the coach roared suddenly, shaking a clenched fist. "Wipe up the ice with them." He shook his fist in the air three times. "Fight! Fight! Fight!"

"Fight! Fight! Fight!" we answered, fists high. "Fight! Fight! Fight!"

"Outlook bright?" Aaron asked, pounding me on the back.

I nodded and headed back to the net, ready to fight with stick and bones.

"Who is that masked man?" Lenny yelled from the stands. I turned to him, waved, and bowed.

Minutes after the third period started, Aaron made a goal and we were ahead again. There was a huge cheer from the crowd and I remembered how great winning feels. Then, Aaron got the puck as it careened out of the face-off, but some giant of a kid from the Trailblazers threw a hip check and banged him into the boards. There was a lot of shuffling around before the whistle blew and it was Aaron who got sent to the penalty box for two minutes.

Suddenly, one of their guys was aiming a slap shot at me. I flung myself on the ice and the puck pounded off my pads. I caught the next one with the edge of my stick. We were sailing.

Then, with about two minutes to go, this Trailblazer kid was heading in for a shot, Aaron buzzing him close like a mosquito. The kid, whirling around, rammed Aaron on the chin with the butt end of his stick. He did it on purpose. I saw it. Aaron's mask lifted up, his head whipped back, and his knees buckled. He staggered a little, moving his head back and forth like he was trying to shake something off. But he kept on skating.

"Aaron's hurt!" I yelled at the high school kid who was refereeing, but my voice just bounced around the rink. The ref must have been picking his nose or something because he didn't even see it happen. And he sure didn't hear me. One of our guys had gotten the puck and everybody was already halfway down the ice. Aaron headed after them, wobbling a little, leaving drops of blood behind him like a Hansel and Gretel trail.

That's what happens when you fight a big guy, I was thinking, when suddenly there was a huge cheer from the stands. Aaron had grabbed the puck and made another goal. The game buzzer sounded. The marshmallow Jets had roasted them. Aaron raised his arms in the air. The Jets screamed, waved their sticks, and hugged each other. The Trailblazers sprayed ice. We'd won, 4 to 2. Horoscope, you're fabulous, I thought.

Then I spotted something. It was there on the ice where Aaron had got hit in the mouth. Even before I was close enough to tell for sure, I knew what it was. I skated over, but I sure didn't want to pick it up. It was a front tooth, pointed root and all, shaped like a long triangle, bloody and gross. That's what good it did him. You go at it with all you've got and they smash your teeth in. It made me so mad I raised my stick and fired, zapping the tooth like it was a small pink puck.

"McDandel," somebody yelled from the stands, "you haven't got the sense you were born with." I lifted up my mask to see who was shouting. It wasn't just Lenny. Somebody was mad.

At the entrance to the ice, Aaron's father, small and wiry like Aaron, was waving his arms at me, shifting from one foot to the other like he was trying to decide which way to head—to Aaron or to me.

"McDandel, find that tooth. You find that tooth or I'll have one of yours for it." Aaron's tooth? He wanted Aaron's tooth? That's weird, I thought. And then I remembered this article I'd seen in the *Chicago Tribune* about some bizarre mother who'd saved all her little kid's baby teeth and stuck them in plaster so they looked like a tiny set of dentures. There was a picture. It was gross. I just stood looking at Mr. Colby, my mouth hanging open.

Aaron slid up to him, opened his mouth, and showed him the empty space. "Move!" Mr. Colby yelled at me.

I moved. But I couldn't even guess where the stupid tooth had gone. A needle in a haystack, a tear in the ocean, a tooth on a hockey rink. I'd zapped it pretty hard.

What good was a bloody tooth anyway? I was tired. It's hard work being a goalie. All I wanted to do was go home, make my gingerbread one last time, and go to bed. Only three days, after all, until I'd be baking it for keeps.

The tooth had disappeared. Everything that looked like a tooth was a sliver of ice. Over in the stands, Aaron was sitting down with his chin in his hands, looking like he was going to throw up. Mr. Colby and a whole bunch of other fathers and their kids were searching for the tooth, too, rushing around on the ice like those little water bugs that skim over ponds in the summertime.

"I found it!" Mr. Colby called at last, holding his arms up high like Aaron had when he'd made a goal. He was standing smack in the middle of the face-off circle. Everybody cheered.

I skated over to Aaron to see how he was and to take my skates off. Lenny was already sitting next to him, helping Aaron with his skates and telling him jokes, trying to cheer him up. Aaron wasn't laughing. He didn't look like he was even listening. His face, usually dark brown, had turned a strange gray, and I wondered if he was going to faint or something. I just sat there for a minute, ready to catch him, and then as I began to unfasten my shin pads, Coach Kenepker came up to us.

"Well, now, Aaron," he said, kneeling down in front of him to talk straight, coach to kid. "You were a great little scrapper tonight. Couldn't have won without you. Make a goal with a tooth knocked out, now that's heart! I know you'll be back next week. When you fall off a horse, climb back on." Aaron, who hadn't fallen off a horse, but had had a tooth knocked out, smiled weakly, and the empty space made him look like he was eight years old.

Mr. Colby hurried in from the ice, holding the tooth carefully by his thumb and forefinger. "I'm going to rinse this off," he said. "Mitch, if you and Lenny hurry, I'll still drop you off. Be ready in two minutes. I've got to get Aaron to the emergency room at the hospital."

Aaron put his hand over his mouth, closed his eyes, and groaned.

As I pulled on my boots, Coach slapped his hand on my shoulder. "Well, McDandel, I hope you cook better than you tend goal." Then he gave me a big hee-haw. "Just having a little fun," he said. "What you cooking in that big contest, anyway?"

"Gingerbread," I said, and started stuffing my gloves and shin pads and helmet and junk into my big green duffle.

"Oh, wonderful," he said, laughing. "Get to take a little trip to the contest with your mother, too, I hear."

"Yes," I told him. "Me and my mom are flying to Miami Beach, Florida, for it Saturday. There'll be a hundred cooks all together."

"Not so many guys going, I bet."

"I don't know," I told him.

Mr. Colby was sprinting back toward us, carrying that tooth like it was made out of ice and was about to melt away. Aaron stood up carefully.

"It's OK, Coach," Lenny said. "They're gonna let Mitch wear a dress."

Mr. Kenepker pretended not to hear. "What'll you get if you win? A nice blue first-prize ribbon?"

Mr. Colby was shouting at us to hurry, but I answered the coach anyway. I'd show him not to smirk at me. "If I win," I yelled, grabbing my bag and stick, "they give me thirty thousand dollars. Fight! Fight! Fight!" I didn't even turn around to see what his face looked like. I knew. Thirty thousand dollars is something.

4
It's a Doggy-Dog World

THE CAR WAS COLD, BUT THEN THE NIGHT WAS, TOO. Freezing rain clicked on the Colbys' station wagon. In the front seat with his dad, Aaron shivered, his hands cupped around his mouth. He hadn't said a word since he'd lost his tooth, so I didn't know if he was mad at me for bashing it around. Lenny and I were hunched in the back seat, our teeth chattering, waiting for Mr. Colby to start the car.

"Mr. Colby, what do you want that tooth for anyway?" Lenny asked. "It was a buck tooth, so now you've found it, the Tooth Fairy'll have to pay a whole dollar for it."

"I need the tooth," Mr. Colby said, "because we're going to put it back in where it came out." He gunned the engine to warm it up. "That way," he went on, "it will grow back in place." He bent over Aaron and held out the tooth, root up. "All right now, Aaron, I want you to open your mouth."

We all gasped at once and stared at him like he was

a madman, Aaron's father or not. It was the first Aaron had heard of it, too, you could tell. He kept his hands around his mouth and moaned like a low fire siren.

I didn't blame him a bit. There he was with a smashed-up mouth and his dad wanted to stick a pointed dead tooth back in its bloody socket. Yuck.

"Aaron, I know what I'm doing." Mr. Colby's voice was low and serious. "The tooth *belongs* there. Now this won't hurt as much as you think. I promise you. Open up." And he started to pry Aaron's hands away.

I covered my eyes, but Aaron must have opened up because I heard him give a yelp like a whipped puppy, and then his father said, "Now hold it in tight just like that. The doctors at the hospital will know exactly what to do. I'll drive very carefully. And whatever you do, don't let go. You might swallow it."

He backed out of the parking place gingerly and edged onto the icy roadway. Lenny and me kept our mouths shut, taking very short breaths, imagining Aaron's tooth in our mouths, and hoping Mr. Colby wouldn't hit a bump or slam into a pothole. For two or three blocks nobody said anything. Aaron kept giving little choked sobs.

Then, all of a sudden, Mr. Colby must have decided to cheer us up and make us relax because he said, very friendly, "Thirty thousand dollars is a lot of money, Mitch. You expect to win it?"

He was worried sick about Aaron's tooth and there

he was talking about my contest. "Sure, I do," I told him. "I'm very confident. My mother says it's not likely, though," I told him nervously, trying not to listen to Aaron. "It's health food gingerbread made with whole-wheat flour mixed with molasses and walnuts and grated carrots and pineapple juice and raisins and stuff." I was talking louder and louder and faster and faster like I couldn't stop. "Not sweet and gooey enough to win, Mom says. She says a lot of people have forgotten what good healthy food tastes like. What do *you* think, Mr. Colby?"

He didn't answer me. He paused for a second at a red light and then turned right onto Central, the street with the hospital on it. "I'm going to drop you boys off at your corner," he said. The station wagon slid to a stop and its back wheels swerved sideways into the curb.

Lenny opened the door and we eased out, pulling all my junk out with us. "Good luck, Aaron," I said quietly, and shut the door as soft as I could so as not to jiggle his tooth. We watched the wheels spin around on the ice before the car finally skidded away down the glassy street. Aaron was slumped down in the front seat so we couldn't even see him.

We looked at each other and Lenny shook his head. "Sounds bananas to me."

"Did you leave your hat in the car?" I asked him. The wind blasting down the street must have been shooting right through his ears. I'd pulled my Black Hawks cap down almost over my eyes, the wind was so fierce.

We started walking. Maybe it was the streetlight, but his ears looked blue. "Oh, I don't need one," he told me. "Besides, I don't have mine. Mom sent it to the cleaners Tuesday. She was afraid to put it in the washer because of the lice thing. I wrote my science report on lice and told her they hold their breath underwater. No joke." He shrugged his shoulders. "They fumigated the whole house today. Boy, is she hysterical."

I'd forgotten Lenny was one of those kids who'd had lice. Every day that week the school nurse had made a big head hunt, searching everybody's hair for lice. Then when the principal gave us this very serious hygiene lecture he said the nurse had discovered more than a dozen kids with them. I didn't know a single one who admitted it. Except Lenny. Nobody knew how they got started.

"What's an ink-pink for frozen head bugs?" I asked him.

Lenny laughed. "Not bad, McDandel," he said. "You stick with me and I'll make a comedian out of you yet. What's an ink-pink for a bug that lives on a rodent's head?"

"Mouse louse," I told him. "Let's run or I'll have a froze nose. Say, you still got those things? Those lice?" I asked as we slid along. If he did, I was going to scoot over about ten inches away from him.

"Listen," he said, panting as we ran, "my head has been scrubbed so clean and rubbed with so much medicine that no self-respecting louse would come near it. Even so, I haven't seen my sister Miriam in days. She won't even talk to me. She thinks lice travel on sound waves."

The sidewalk was as slick as an ice rink, so Lenny grabbed my stick and slapped an empty Good and Plenty box with it. I ran ahead, kicked it a good whack, and we passed it back and forth all the way down the block to the steps of my house. Lenny lives two blocks east of me, near the university where his folks work. He decided to stop in and de-ice.

Inside the front hall it was warm and smelled like applesauce. Mom and Dad were sitting at the dining room table with the supper dishes just stacked up and pushed to the middle. They were drinking rose hip tea and working over the checkbook and a stack of papers—money work, a big, fat pain.

"Hi, troops," Dad said, pushing the bills away, "and how were the aptly named Jets?"

"Like the cheese," Lenny said, "they stand alone."

"Winner and still champion," I told him. "But Aaron lost a tooth making two points."

Lenny went through the whole thing, acting it all

out from the stick in the mouth to the tooth in the gum. "You really think they can paste it back in?" he asked.

"Shall I call his mother to let her know, do you think?" Mom asked.

Lenny shook his head. "It was all so crazy I feel like I made it up. Let them tell her."

"Poor Aaron," Mom said. She erased some numbers on the yellow pad in front of her and shook her head. "He just wasn't cut out to be a hockey player." She sighed. "Like I wasn't cut out to run a store." At first I thought she was going to cry. Mom is like that when they get everything together to pay the bills. She groans a lot. But she laughed instead and said, "At least I still have my teeth." Sunshine didn't use to make her so down. I remember when I was in the third and fourth grades how excited she was teaching big bunches of people how to cook with natural foods. And then those people in her classes would come in asking questions and buying supplies and it was all like a big friendly party. This year she'd cut out giving classes. "I need a rest," she'd said.

"Well, what's it doing out there?" Dad asked cheerfully, like he wanted to change the subject.

We threw our boots on the rubber mat by the door.

"On the six o'clock news Leroi Rupert said we had a thirty-percent chance of precipitation tonight," I told him. "It's raining one-hundred percent ice. Can't trust even the world's best disc jockey with the weather."

"Have some trail mix, you guys," Mom said. She pushed over a dish filled with nuts, dried apricots, dates, coconut chips, and other good things. "You must be starving after combat."

Trail mix was just what I needed. Dad made it himself at the store. He did all the ordering of supplies for Sunshine and really liked talking to the people who came in wanting us to stock their stuff. But, no matter how hard they tried to sell it to him, he wouldn't buy anybody else's trail mix. I was as hungry as if I'd been on the trail for three days so I scooped out a handful and tossed it in my mouth. Lenny fingered through the bowl and picked out the nuts, eating them one by one, clearly not trusting the soybeans, sunflower seeds, banana chips, and other things he didn't know.

Mom narrowed her eyes and watched him pick.

Lenny saw her watching and smiled. "Say, Mrs. McDandel," he said, crunching away, "do you know which nuts always make me sneeze?"

"Lenny, I didn't know you were allergic." She turned over the yellow pad she'd been figuring on and looked at Lenny with concern. When he grinned, she said, "Lenny Barker, this isn't a joke is it?"

"Ah . . . ah . . . AH . . . *cashews*!" Lenny sneezed,

and we all laughed but Mom. I even laugh at Lenny's worst jokes, which is probably why we've been friends so long.

"Listen, it's almost eight o'clock, I can't stay," Lenny said, throwing his coat on a chair and going over to our little upright piano in the living room. He sat down and started playing the "Maple Leaf Rag." He'd played it the week before at the sixth-grade talent show. He played it very fast and very loud.

When he stopped, I leaned over and asked him, "Why do you always have to tell my mom jokes? You know how it bugs her."

"Elementary, my dear McGingerbread. I tell her jokes because she has this weird idea that just because I'm not a health food freak I'm a fast food freak. And if I didn't tell her jokes, I think she'd lose her faith that sugar and hot dogs rot your brain."

"She really does think you're hyper."

"Sure, I'm hyper. Hyper, my friend, means super, and that's me all over. I also eat liver and spinach," he whispered, "but don't breathe it to a soul." He cupped his hands together and blew to warm them up. "And now on to a little prize-winning Mozart."

He's a really good piano player, Lenny is. His dad teaches oboe at the university and he makes Lenny practice before school and after, too. That kind of hours and I guess you either get good or you go bonkers.

"Listen, you think *you*'ve got a contest coming up," he said. "I've got a really big one next month. I'm going to wipe out those weak-fingered kids in a concerto audition. The one that wins gets to play with the Evanston Philharmonia this spring. What's your thirty thousand dollars compared to *that*, I ask you?" And he played a few bars of his big contest piece.

"More, Lenny, more," Mom called from the dining room when he stopped. "That's lovely. Doesn't it make you proud to play like that?" She waited a minute for him to say something. "And don't you dare answer me with a joke."

Lenny laughed. "Come on. I had one ready. Sure you don't want to hear it? It's Dad's joke. Very high quality."

"Absolutely sure," she said, appearing in the living room with her fingers in her ears. Lenny watched until she took them out and then started talking. "Why do I feel so bad when I play the piano alone . . . ?"

"Mitch," she called to me, raising her voice like she does when she gets mad. "Mitch, aren't you going to make that gingerbread?"

Then Lenny got louder than she was. "Why do I feel so bad when I play the piano alone, you ask? Because I'm solo. I feel so *low*, get it?"

Mom laughed. "Leonard Barker, I'm convinced all those jokes are a symptom of sugar poisoning."

Mitch gave me an I-told-you-so look and laughed with her.

"Come on, didn't I help Mitch name his fancy gingerbread?" Lenny asked. "He's going to give me a thousand of that thirty when he wins it. That's how much he likes the name."

"You haven't even tasted it," she said.

"I've seen a list of what's in it and that's enough for me."

I looked up to see if he meant it like that. But when he saw me looking, he coughed and smiled broadly. "I mean, enough for me to make up a brilliant name."

"Lenny," Dad asked him, "how much do you have to practice to play like that?"

"I play four or eight hours a day, whichever comes first. Enough so I miss eighty-six percent of the really good stuff on TV. Gary Conrad had a guy on his show last night who'd climbed up the Statue of Liberty and sat on the torch for three hours, and I missed it." He shrugged.

"That program," Mom said, "has virtually no redeeming value. I mean, if you were a Pulitzer Prize winner wouldn't you resent being on a show with somebody whose sole talent was writing her name on her back holding the pen between her toes? I've got to believe, Lenny, that playing your scales is better than watching Gary Conrad."

Dad got up and stretched. He looked over at the

47

pile of bills on the table and slapped the checkbook shut.

"No kidding, you practice four hours a day?" Dad sat down on the piano bench next to Lenny, scooted him over, and started to noodle around on the keys. "One hour a day used to be my limit." Then he started playing some old-timey stuff—"Sunny Side of the Street," "Jada," and "Ugly Chile." I loved it when he sang that one.

"Sing it," I asked him. "It's a Lenny kind of song."

He grinned and looked over at my mom. He used to tell me how he'd played it for her before they got married. "Some courtship tune," she'd tell him.

It's funny, they'd met in a place called Zounds!, a tiny natural food store in Chicago. He was the clerk in the morning before going to his college classes. She was the clerk in the afternoon and night. So that was the business they knew best and when they got married they saved up and borrowed so they could start their own natural food store. It took three years. Mom stayed on at Zounds! Dad worked lots of jobs. Nights he was a cab driver, weekends he was a house painter, and during the days he was a teller in a bank, which Mom says he hated. He named the new store Sunshine because, he said, it made him as warm and happy as the sun to be his own boss in his own store. That was ten years ago.

Now, he played a long glissando on the piano.

"All you're going to do is give Lenny more material," Mom warned. And it was true. Lenny made him go over it until he knew the words and could play it by ear.

> You're knock-kneed, pigeon-toed,
> Box-ankled, too.
> There's a curse on your family,
> And it fell on you.
> Hey! you're ugly, man, you're ugly.
> You're some ugly chile.

It was even better when Lenny sang it. He's the fartherest thing from ugly. I mean, girls call him all the time. When he was a little kid his mom used to take him to Chicago to see if people in the advertising agencies would use him as a curly-headed blond model to sell breakfast cereal and toys and stuff. For a while he worked, but then, his mother said, he wouldn't sit still long enough, so she gave it up. When we were in third grade Lenny's picture was on a big billboard. He was talking on the telephone. The idea was to get people to call their grandmothers long distance like that cute little kid was doing. The billboard was right in the middle of downtown Evanston, and Lenny got a whole bunch of us kids to go over one rainy day and we all threw mud balls at it. It took a huge blob to cover just one tooth, that's how big it was.

"You like playing?" Dad asked him. "You must."

"Who likes practicing?" Lenny said, running his fingers over the keys. "Actually, my dad says music is going to be my free ride to college. It's a doggy-dog world out there, he says, so you've got to make plans how you're going to make it."

"Dog-*eat*-dog," Mom said, lying down on the sofa and propping her feet up on a pillow. "Sometimes I think I'm the dog that's being eaten. It's competition he's talking about, dog-eat-dog competition."

"No, *doggy*-dog," Lenny went on. "It just means getting ahead. What's wrong with that?"

"What's he talking college for, anyway?" Mom asked. "That's eons away. You're just twelve."

"Twelve and a half," Lenny told her. "Next year he says I'm going to start the trumpet, and when I'm in high school I'll take the French horn so, he says, if I win enough music competitions, the colleges will come looking for me. You've got to have an ace in the hole, he says, and that'll be mine."

"Dog-eat-dog," Mom said, pulling herself to her feet. "Come on, Ralph, we don't want to be late."

"Where you going?" I asked her. "It's awful outside."

"Not fit for doggy-dog," Lenny said.

"Nothing important, just a meeting," Dad told me, stacking up the papers on the dining room table and putting them in his briefcase.

"You think we'll need all those?" Mom asked.

"We'll be driving, it won't be so bad. Get your coat on, Lenny, and we'll drop you off."

As Lenny pulled on his boots I asked Dad, "Is the meeting about Sunshine? What's happening? Tell me. I mean, you're always saying that Sunshine is one-third mine."

"Oh, it's nothing," he said. "Don't you worry. You go in and make that famous gingerbread so it'll be perfect Sunday, and everything will be all right."

"Get to bed on time, now. We'll try not to be late," Mom told me.

"Where are you going?" I asked her.

"See you," she said.

After the door closed, I trudged into the kitchen to make my gingerbread for school. It would be the last time before the Bakeathon. Coach Kenepker was right, too, I thought. I had to be a whole lot better baker than I was a goalie if I was going to win that one. I wanted to be doggy-dog. I wanted to win. I wanted to put big numbers in our checkbook, numbers that would wipe out Mom's grumps and give Dad cash to stock the shelves.

As I measured out the flour I thought about Mr. Corso's offer, and then I got this great idea that with the thirty thousand dollars maybe Mom and Dad and I could start a whole chain of Sunshines. In my head I could see the signs clearly—big, bright orange with the sun's rays in yellow, sitting right next to signs for McDonald's and Pizza Hut and Poppin' Fresh Pies. We'd sell takeout health food, and first on the menu would be Mitch McDandel's Health Nutty Ginger-bread.

5

Yuck!

EVERY WEEKDAY MORNING AT EIGHT-TWENTY-FIVE, AARON and Lenny and me meet at the corner of Central and Ashland to catch the bus to school. Friday I left the house early because I had to carry a baking pan filled with the gingerbread I'd made the night before. I kept wishing I'd baked it that morning so the pan would still be warm against my hands. Under my arm I'd tucked a package with white napkins and a yellow folder with my report on the foods of ancient Rome. The report was due Monday, but I wasn't going to be at school then. I was going to be on my way home from the Royal Imperial Towers hotel in sunny, hot Miami Beach, Florida. Tan and rich.

The wind was still spinning the treetops around like mixers and the sky was gray as smoke. Monica Darling, a sixth-grade kid who lives next door to me, was already there, looking warm in her green down jacket. She wasn't wearing a hat, so either all that long blond hair kept her ears warm or her mother was washing it because she had lice like Lenny. She was carrying a shoe-box diorama book report. That's when you make a scene from a book inside a box. They do that in Mr. Rowe's class. In Mrs. Archer's room we write I-like-this-book-because reports. Dioramas are baby stuff.

"You like it?" she asked, holding it out so I could see. "It's the cave in Hannibal, Missouri, that Tom Sawyer and Becky Thatcher hid in when Injun Joe was after them." I looked in the little end of the box and saw two crayon-drawn kids at the back sticking their heads up behind brown construction-paper rocks. Behind another rock up front she'd stuck a feather. Injun Joe. "You think I'll get an A for it?" she asked.

"Yeah, sure," I lied. "That's really very interesting."

"What have you got?" she asked. "It smells good."

"Just some gingerbread," I told her, shrugging like it was nothing. I wondered how it was going to taste frozen, if the bus didn't come pretty soon. It smelled good enough to make me hungry, even though I'd just finished a big bowl of granola. It was the sweet smell of molasses, ginger, and thirty thousand dollars.

Lenny came running, twirling an orange cap on his finger, just as the bus rounded the corner. He's got almost three blocks to run from his house. The bus begins its route a block from our stop, so it's never late. But if we're even a minute late, it means a mile-and-a-half dash across town. Aaron wasn't anywhere in sight. I knew I should have called him to see how he was, but I was too chicken.

"OK, you guys, move it," Marie said as she opened the bus door. She's always telling us to move it, like we weren't practically frozen and dying to move it into her super-heated bus.

"How's my Darling?" Lenny said to Monica as he snaked in ahead of us, not breaking out of his gallop. Monica didn't even roll her eyes. People are always calling her that. If it was my name, I'd change it.

"How'd you like to wear my cap today, Darling?" Lenny said to her as he passed, waving it back and forth in front of her face.

She narrowed her eyes. "You come near me with that buggy thing and I'll go straight to the principal and my father will sue you for all you're worth." Then she plunked herself down in a window seat near the back because she knew we would sit in the far back. She was close enough to talk but too far for lice to jump.

"Where'd you get that hat?" I asked Lenny.

"It's new," he said. "My dad brought it home last night." He called over to Monica, "If it's lousy we're taking it back to the Sports Shop."

We sat down in the middle of the long bench at the back of the bus. We always sit there. It's our throne because we're the best, because we're sixth graders and next year we'll be in junior high. But mostly it's ours because we're the first ones on and nobody else can get there before us.

I looked out the back window to see if Aaron was just running late and I could yell and tell Marie to stop the bus and wait. But he wasn't. Only the wind was rushing.

All the way to school Lenny told kids about the night before. "Did you guys hear about Aaron?" he'd ask, and none of them had. Every time he told the story it got bigger and wilder and bloodier, and by the time the bus rolled past the crossing guards in front of Lincoln School, he was telling another kid about how this six-foot hulk had rammed his fist into Aaron's mouth and how I came running out to fight, leaving my goal untended, and how, while I was gone, the Trailblazers had slapped both the puck and Aaron's tooth into the net. "The question is," he was saying as the bus pulled up in front of school, "should the Trailblazers really have gotten that extra point for the tooth?"

Most of the kids just groaned and got up to leave. They knew Lenny and his stories. Monica said, very coolly, that she bet Aaron missed the bus because he was too busy watching the Three Stooges on TV.

"OK, you guys, move it," Marie shouted. She must say it in her sleep. "Pick up your feet. Don't leave anything on the bus."

There was a big jam-up at the door. I was still in

back, holding the gingerbread close to keep it from getting smooshed. People *weren't* moving. They were standing on the steps staring down at something. Guarding my gingerbread, I eased into a window seat to see what it was.

I should have known. It was Aaron, looking alive, after Lenny had just finished telling them he was nothing but a mass of pulp. His mother must have brought him in the car. He was standing right by the bus door waiting for Lenny and me to get out. Kids started edging down the steps and peering at him. Sure enough, his top lip was swollen and purple, but his face was brown again, and not that ashy gray it was when I saw him last. You couldn't see his teeth because he wasn't smiling. I guess the kids from the bus started to believe Lenny's story the minute they saw how Aaron's lip looked. They were pressing up against him, bombing him with questions about this six-foot forward who beat him up and how many teeth did he really lose and stuff. By the time Lenny and I got off the bus, they had backed Aaron up ten feet. He wasn't used to being treated like a rock star with twenty-four gold records.

"Step aside, folks," I said, prodding them a little with my gingerbread pan. "We're Mr. Colby's body-guards. He's not giving any interviews today and no autographs."

Lenny grabbed him by the arm and we rushed inside together. Aaron was tight as a clam. As we climbed the steps to the sixth-grade hall, Lenny couldn't wait any longer to ask him the big question. "Did they do it? Did they really glue your old tooth back in? You didn't swallow it on the way to the hospital, did you?"

Aaron turned to us and grinned. Actually, it was more like he was baring his teeth at us. And it looked strange. It looked really strange. Three of his front teeth were covered with white stuff so hard, thick, and shiny that it looked like he had one tooth that was three teeth wide. Nothing was missing. There was too much there.

"What *is* that?" I gasped. He looked like a beaver.

"Is it like that forever?" Lenny asked him. "I never saw anything like that before in my life."

"It's a splint," Aaron said, grinning like he was proud of it, "just like you get on your leg if you break it. It's a tooth splint." He stuck his crazy teeth over his bottom lip and rubbed his finger over the big one. "It's hard plastic like they make fake teeth with and it anchors the tooth that came out to the two teeth next to it. That's what the doctor said last night. It's reimplanted." We stopped on the landing and stared.

"What did your mother say?" I asked him. I'd wondered about his mother a lot when I lay in bed thinking about slapping his tooth across the ice.

"She said she knew it would happen sometime,"

Aaron said, shaking his head. "And I guess she did, because it did happen and she always said it would. My dad said it was a freak accident, but my mother said that hockey is a freak game and she forbids me absolutely to play it anymore. My dad said the same thing Coach Kenepker said about getting back on a horse after it's thrown you."

"Maybe you should just take up horseback riding. No kidding," Lenny asked, "what are you going to do?"

"I'm sure not gonna quit," he said. "And the bigger I get, the better I'll get. But," he went on, "Thursdays at our house are going to be very sticky."

We climbed the rest of the way upstairs and kids from the bus started hanging around us. Aaron raised his voice, not really talking to Lenny and me anymore. "The splint stays on six weeks like a cast on a broken bone," he said like he was a tour guide, turning his smile around so everyone could see. "The doctor said they save ninety percent of knocked-out teeth if they get them back in within a half hour." He beamed at his audience. "We may have been a little over that. So what!" He shrugged. "Maybe after all this splinting it'll turn green and fall out, but the doctor says there's a good chance we'll save it."

By the time we reached our lockers, kids were all over him like he was a hero. He loved it. He didn't even notice when I headed off toward Mrs. Archer's room with the gingerbread. I heard Monica ask him, "Did it hurt a lot when the dentist put it back in?"

"Actually, it was a doctor who put it in," Aaron told her. "In the emergency room at the hospital. It was an emergency implantation." They disappeared into Mr. Rowe's room.

When Mrs. Archer walked into class the gingerbread and a package of napkins were in the middle of her desk. She stood in front of it and took a good deep breath. "Oh, that's a glorious smell," she said. "I don't know if I can wait." After she'd called the roll, she said, "I have absolutely no willpower. Why don't we all sample the gingerbread now and Mitch can tell us about the recipe and how he's going to win a contest with it."

I hadn't figured on making a speech. I'm not good at that, but there didn't seem to be any way out of it. I walked up to the front of the room and stood near Mrs. Archer's desk where the gingerbread was. While she lifted out slices onto the white napkins I'd brought, I told the class that I enter contests all the time. When I was eight I won a camera in the Red Bell Raisins sweepstakes. Of course, that was the *only* contest I'd won, but it was enough to keep me going. Then, a couple of months ago, I'd found an entry blank for the ABC Bakeathon contest in the baking soda I was using. I told the kids how for years I'd taken Mom's cooking lessons at Sunshine and that I cook supper at home a lot and how I just took that entry blank and made up a natural food gingerbread for it. I explained how I'd tried it out and it was pretty good so I showed the recipe to Lenny and he'd given it a name. I never thought I'd be one of the one hundred finalists, though. I was just explaining how five winners would get a thousand dollars and three winners would get five thousand dollars and the grand prize winner would get *thirty* thousand dollars, and I was getting all ready to smile modestly as they said, "Oh, wow, thirty thousand dollars!" when Mrs. Archer started handing out samples and people started tasting it.

Debby Jaynes, who sits in the front row, took a bite first, screwed up her mouth, turned to the girl next to her, and said—loud enough so I could hear—"Yuck!" I looked over at Lenny, who smiled up at me, took a bite, gagged, and forced himself to swallow.

"It doesn't have any sugar in it," I explained. "Just molasses. That's why it's not as sweet as you're probably used to. It's naturally sweetened with molasses and pineapple juice and raisins and grated carrots." A boy in the back of the room spit his piece into his napkin.

I was ready to give up the whole dumb Bakeathon right then until a kid leaned over and said, "It's not so bad." Maybe, I thought, you had to practically grow up on health food to like my gingerbread.

"Class," Mrs. Archer said sharply, "your teasing is rude. Quiet down this minute." She took a small bite of the gingerbread. "It's delicious," she said, without wincing. "Are these walnuts?"

That's when the sirens started. In great waves of sound they roared past, like it was all the emergency equipment Evanston had, pouring by our school.

"They're ambulances," Debby said to Tasha, the girl next to her. "They're coming to take us away to have our stomachs pumped." It was one of those jokes that spread around the room fast, and the more sirens that roared by, the more people laughed about the poisoned gingerbread. I stood there looking at them, trying to figure out some easy way to get to my seat in the back.

"What's the recipe's name, Mitch?" Mrs. Archer asked loudly, trying to get everybody's attention without embarrassing me by having to shush them again.

"Lenny named it Health Nutty Gingerbread," I said. Everybody roared.

"People, you'll spend five minutes after school in total silence if this behavior doesn't stop," Mrs. Archer said over the din. When everyone had quieted down and all the sirens had stopped and all the gingerbread-filled napkins had been thrown into the wastebasket, Mrs. Archer said it was time to finish up the science reports on animals.

"Then, Monday, you know," she said, "your Social

Studies reports are due on ancient Rome. I hope you haven't left them to the last minute. Mitch has already turned his in."

Lenny leaned over and whispered to me, "You luck, I don't even know what to write mine on."

There were three more animal reports left. Karen Gould gave hers on the prairie dog, which she said was a small, cute creature that wasn't a dog, but was an endangered species because so many farmers were trying to kill it. Then Debby Jaynes, the one who'd said "yuck" first, gave hers on the spotted leopard, which, it turned out, was also in danger of extinction.

Then it was Lenny's turn. He had a batch of cards to read from. See, Lenny studies a whole lot more than he pretends to. I don't know why he wants people to think he's a dodo, but he does.

One of the girls had talked like a machine gun. The other had stared at the floor. Lenny stood up and held out this grotesque picture of a monster-looking creature he'd drawn with Magic Marker on a piece of typing paper. He didn't say what it was. "I bet you didn't know George Washington had lice," he said. People started to laugh nervously. "A lot of famous people had lice. *I* had lice." There were giggles. "They are definitely not an endangered species, even though man keeps trying to make them extinct.

"Monkeys eat their own lice," he went on, and everybody gagged. They'd all heard the big personalhygiene lecture the principal had given two days before about how lice carry diseases, and they'd all had their heads searched by the nurse. "In the Orient they eat flied lice," Lenny said with a straight face, and nobody got it but me, because I'd heard him say it before.

"There are two kinds of lice," he told us. "One is the biting kind. They live in feathers and hair and they each have their own special kind of animal they live on. Like, there are pigeon lice and chicken lice and turkey lice. If a turkey louse has bad eyes or something and lands on a goose, he'll right away try chewing on the goose's feathers, but he won't be able to stand the taste. Once a turkey louse, always a turkey louse."

Lenny looked down at his cards. Kids started glancing at the back of each other's heads to see if they could locate any bugs. "The other kind is the sucking kind," Lenny went on, and the kids stared back at him, trying to figure out if he was trying to be funny or not. "They suck blood like vampires would if there really were vampires, which, for all I know, there are. But that's another report."

He checked his cards again. "There are 225 kinds of sucking lice, like dog lice, cat lice, goat lice, horse lice, and people lice. That's what we had—people lice." When he looked around the room it was like he *knew* if there had been Barbara lice and Joshua lice and Rodney lice. I mean, some people started looking down at the floor and turning red. "You can't catch lice from your dog because dog lice don't eat people.

"People lice are called *Pediculus humanus capitis,*" he said, pointing to the words at the bottom of the picture he'd drawn. "They have this huge stomach, six legs with claws on them, and a drill so they can burrow in and suck your blood."

"Oh, gross," somebody said.

"It gets better," Lenny went on. "They've got this kind of saliva that they spit on the hole they've drilled and that's what makes your head itch." Just like he'd turned loose a whole famished army of lice, everybody in the room started to scratch their heads and then look under their fingernails to see if a vampire with a drill was there, ready to spit at them.

"They're as easy to catch as a cold. All you've got to do is wear the hat of somebody who has them or use their comb, or like that. And if you try to get rid of them just by washing your hair with plain shampoo, you can't because the louse just seals off his air holes and holds his breath until your head is dry again. You've got to use bug-killer shampoo."

Then he finished by saying, "Due to the miracle of modern science, I have destroyed my own private home for lice, and I hope the rest of you have, too."

He crumpled up the picture of the bug and arced it across the room toward the wastebasket. He made it. Everybody clapped.

What a nut. Nobody else in the whole class would have given that crazy report. Nobody. They'd have died first, but Lenny really likes it when people laugh.

I was staring at Mrs. Archer's desk, where the rest of my gingerbread sat, when she came up behind me, leaned down, and said, "Mitch, there's somebody outside who wants to talk to you." She said it soft and kind of somber, and I thought it probably had something to do with the recipe and how awful it was.

But it wasn't that. In the hall where she pointed, I could see Leroi Rupert. In person. Leroi Rupert is this wild disc jockey on radio station WOGR and he's a friend of me and my family. He always bought food from Sunshine and all, even after the supermarket moved so close. *He'd* have liked the gingerbread. He's wonderful and very funny over the air, very big on monsters. He'd have loved the lice report.

Leroi was standing back from the door so most of the kids couldn't see him. If they had, they'd have gone bonkers. I couldn't imagine what he wanted me for, but I went out anyway, feeling happy again, because Leroi Rupert is a really good guy.

Once I got in the hall, I said, "Hi, Leroi, how'd I get to be this lucky? I wasn't even the thirteenth caller or . . ." And then I realized he wasn't going to smile. He wasn't there to smile. It looked like something was terribly wrong.

"Mitch," he said, very quiet. And then he paused. And I knew for sure something was wrong.

He must have seen me panic. "Your folks are all right," he said fast, so I couldn't have time to imagine any awful stuff.

Then what was wrong? It was all over his face that there was something he didn't want to tell me. "It's Sunshine," he said. "You must have heard the sirens. Your folks were just opening when they smelled the smoke. The fire started in the back of the store, so they weren't hurt."

I kept moving my mouth, but not thinking of any words to fill it with.

"I saw the fire from the radio station," he went on. "By nine-thirty there were huge billows of smoke, but even from the thirteenth floor I could tell it was Sunshine that was burning."

"Sunshine burning," I repeated after him. In my head I couldn't imagine smoke and Sunshine. "Have you been there?" I asked. I had a hard time catching my breath, like some guy had rammed my stomach with a hockey stick.

"Yes, yes, I have. I saw it. Listen, Mitch, your folks are very strong people, you know that. They're doing

OK. But they didn't feel they should leave. They asked me to come over and tell you. Your dad didn't want you just to find out from some kid who walked up and said, 'Did you hear about Sunshine?' "

6
Did You Hear About Sunshine?

WE WENT ROARING TO THE FIRE IN LEROI RUPERT'S WOGR van. It looked official so nobody stopped us for speeding, but I bet we were pushing fifty in a thirty-mile zone. Leroi had got me out of school even though my principal didn't like the idea at all. Mr. Jager said that not only was it dangerous, but it would give me bad dreams, besides. But Leroi said my parents had insisted that I come, that my dad had said it was a family business and that I was a third of the family. So Mr. Jager let me go. I wonder if he would have done it for anybody but famous, cool, Leroi Rupert, 1440 on your AM radio dial?

Sunshine was in the middle of the block, but the whole street was closed to traffic. Fire trucks and police cars were parked at angles across it, so we had to leave the van two blocks away and run back. Ropes crisscrossed the sidewalk in front of the store, but there weren't any flames that I could see. Just outside the smashed-in front window a single fireman stood

69

spraying water where the bread rack used to be. His yellow slicker was streaked with gray smoke and black soot. Why did firemen stop wearing red? I wondered.

Mom and Dad weren't there. I'd expected to see them out fighting the fire, too, saving things like heroes do. Two firemen, their faces all smudged, were coiling up a hose that lay in the street. Held back by the rope, we stood there with the crowd, searching for my folks. I almost didn't want to see them because I could tell how bad it really was. Inside, everything was black. Total eclipse of Sunshine. The family business. All three thirds of it gone.

"Do you suppose they saved anything?" I asked Leroi. The metal pipes that used to hold the yellow awning had melted down. Except for a few black shreds, the yellow awning was gone, too.

"Not unless they grabbed it as they ran out," he said. "I don't think they've been inside since. Listen, Mitch, I'm going to look for a policeman to find out where your folks are. I'm due back for the noon news. Want to come along to look?"

"No," I told him. "Please. I just want to stay here by the lamppost and watch. Tell them I'm by the lamppost." He gave me a broad Leroi smile and went off looking. I wondered if Sunshine would be on the noon news.

Moving away from the post, I pressed in against the rope as far as I could. The dark, sour smell gagged you even worse close up. Strips of black wood and bubbled plastic were all that was left of the check-out counter. The cash register looked like you'd never want to touch it again. The old pressed-metal ceiling with patterns on it that Mom liked so much hung down in wide, ragged strips. Its edges had curled up with the flames.

Part of the smell was charred food—burned organic tomatoes and sprouts just delivered yesterday. How hot did it have to get to burn through a refrigerator? And where was my peanut butter machine? I almost couldn't make my head think about it. The machine really was mine. I always worked it. When I made myself look over to check, I couldn't see a thing. The back part of the store had caved in.

When I was little I wanted to be a fireman. I liked their hats and the way the firemen hung on to the side of the engine when it tilted around corners. But now I didn't see how they could stand it. The smell choked me. It wasn't a campfire smell at all. It filled up my nose and then my lungs and made my eyes water worse than chopped onions do. It would make you cry even if you didn't feel like crying anyway because of all the stuff turning black and disappearing in front of your eyes.

As I watched, the fireman who was squirting water on the store turned around. He thought I was just some neighbor kid who liked to watch fires. He smiled, nodded, and blew a huge bubble from the wad of green gum he was working on.

Just as the bubble got so big I was sure it was going to break all over his face, Mom came up behind me and gave me a hug. Dad put his hand on my shoulder and said, "It's OK, Mitch, we'll be all right," and I remembered he'd said it the night before, too.

"Sorry to run," Leroi told us, "but I've got a show to do. I'm sure not going to be funny this afternoon. It's heavy," he said. "In every sense, it's heavy. If I can do anything . . . ?"

"You already have," Dad told him as he shook his hand. "Thanks."

Mom took his hand in both of hers and smiled. Leroi smiled back, turned, and sprinted off.

Then, just like he'd been interrupted in the middle of a sentence, the tall, thin fireman who'd walked up with them started talking. "—seemed just to explode. We couldn't get near it, it was so intense. What was back there anyway? A batch of aerosol cans? Sometimes that'll set it off."

"We don't carry aerosol cans," Mom told him. Then she corrected herself. "Didn't carry aerosol cans." She looked over at Dad and then back to the fireman. "They endanger the upper atmosphere," she explained softly.

"Well, I tell you, we couldn't have done a whole

lot more to save it, Mrs. McDandel. Looks like it may have been smoldering all night long before it finally took hold. No signs of forced entry."

The fire chief came up and joined them. It said "Chief" on his white slicker, and he was smoking a big fat cigar. He probably thought it smelled better than the fire, but I sure didn't. "Well, I'm afraid that's that," he said. "After we soak it down a bit more, we're going to pack up and go. I hope your insurance was paid up, at least, McDandel." He blew out a cloud of smoke and my mother winced.

"Oh, yes," Dad said. "We're pretty well covered by insurance. And again, thank you. You did all that could be done and more. We'll be all right now."

"All right." He'd said it again. And "covered by insurance," he'd said, too. Did that mean we wouldn't have to go on welfare or anything? The store was all gone but the money wasn't, was that it? I felt better, like it was easier to breathe, but I wished I knew exactly what "covered by insurance" meant.

"Probably you folks realize there'll be an arson squad going to work back there just as soon as it's safe for them to do so," the chief said casually, taking a big puff on his cigar. "How's tomorrow morning sound to you?"

My mother looked pale. She's allergic to cigar smoke. I wanted to tell him to put it out, but he was the fire chief and I was scared to.

"Of course," Dad said. Mom moved away from the cigar, her eyes watering.

"We do it automatically," the chief went on. "How about ten o'clock tomorrow morning? Can you meet us then, McDandel?"

"Fine," Dad said. "We want to know what caused the fire as much as you do. But I doubt it was arson."

"What's arson?" I asked, and they all looked at me like they hadn't known I was there. Then they started stammering around as if arson was a dirty word or something from an X-rated movie that a kid wasn't supposed to ask about. I wished I hadn't said anything.

"Uh, arson," the first fireman said, clearing his throat, "is when somebody sets a fire on purpose, sometimes just because they're crazy or mean, sometimes to collect the insurance money to cover their debts. Now, we don't think anybody did that . . ." He chuckled nervously and smiled a smile that went up and down fast. ". . . but we have to check it out. Arson is a crime, and the police would want to apprehend anybody who did it. OK?"

"OK," I said. I didn't understand why everybody seemed so uncomfortable.

"So we have a special squad that checks each fire out," the chief went on. "It's like a big puzzle, a fire like this one. We can't tell what happened in there," and he pointed at what was left of Sunshine with what was left of his big cigar. "Well, goodbye," he said to my folks. "Sorry about your loss."

As they walked away, Mom turned to Dad. Her neck was all tight and splotched with red and she looked scared. "They think we set the fire, Ralph. They think *we* did it."

He started to rub the back of her neck. "Sarah, it's been a killing day, but you can't let it get you down. They don't think anything of the sort." She hung her head and let him rub.

Arson is a crime, the chief had said. I followed along behind him and the tall fireman, close enough to listen to what they were saying. There was a crowd of people wandering around and asking each other questions about how the fire started and when, and pushing in to get a better look, so the two men didn't notice me following them.

"What do you think?" I heard the chief ask.

"I don't know," the tall fireman said, bending down toward him. "There are some things that look suspicious back there. They may not mean a thing, of course. I don't know. It was a bad one all right." They took a few steps without saying anything.

"How were they doing financially with the store, did you find out?" the chief asked him.

"Breaking even, McDandel told me, but I'd guess it's worse than that. There's that Stop and Save that opened up a block away, and it's going great guns."

"Must have hurt this place," the chief said. "But that's no excuse for arson. It's a dog-eat-dog world, even for health food crazies." The chief tossed his cigar into a pool of water and blew out his breath like it tasted stale. "Some fools think they can just burn up their losses, collect cash from the insurance company, and go scot-free." His laugh sounded like a bark.

All of a sudden I realized it was cold. I felt tired. It was noon and I was hungry. I sat down on the curb and that's where I was when Mom and Dad found me, watching the firemen clean up. They tried to get me to go home or back to school, even, but I couldn't leave. Dad went over and got some sandwiches and stuff from the deli at the supermarket and he and I ate while Mom paced back and forth in front of the store. Dad's shoulders sagged. "I'm especially sorry about the peanut butter maker," he said to me. "I remember the day you learned how to operate that. You were seven."

"Was the recipe for your trail mix in there?" I asked him, nodding over toward the store.

"Oh, no," he said gently, "it's all in my head. Poor Sunshine." He took a bite of banana and smiled sadly. "I guess this does mean your mom will have some time off. She needed that, I think."

Pretty soon a fireman came over and told Mom and Dad they could look around in the store, that it was safe. I didn't even ask if I could come along.

Hours later I was still sitting on the curb watching two men who'd driven around the police blockade in their red truck. It said "Globe Emergency Enclosures" on the side. They were hammering up huge plywood sheets across the broken windows when Lenny and Aaron came running up. School was out and instead of taking the move-it-guys bus they'd headed straight to the fire. Somebody at school had told them. I wondered who it was who'd finally said, "Did you hear about Sunshine?"

We looked inside before the guys finished boarding the place up. Mom and Dad were still sifting around through the black rubble, not finding much. Nothing was worth taking. Outside on the sidewalk Mr. Corso was standing with his arms crossed, waiting for them.

Dad saw what was coming and tried to change direction and steer Mom away from him, but Mr. Corso ran a little toward them and put his hand out.

"Leaving the scene of the crime?" he asked sarcastically. "You two didn't just happen to put the torch to this failing business, did you? Use a little timer to set something off? Are you sure, Mrs. McDandel, you were going out *for* business?"

"What's he talking about?" Aaron asked me. He looked like somebody had slapped him.

Probably I'd have felt like that, too, but I'd already had my slap in the face when the fireman talked. "Oh, you know," I told him, "Mr. Corso and Mom are always arguing. It doesn't mean anything."

"It's not funny, if that's what he thinks," Lenny said. "They just had their store burn down and he asks if they're the ones that lit the match! That's sick."

"Corso, you know that's ridiculous," Dad said.

"No, I don't. What I know is my brand-new place is a mess and it's your fault. It's going to cost me a mint to put it back in shape." He pressed the palms of his hands against his eyes and rubbed. "I don't know if it will ever stop stinking from your foul health food smoke."

Mom's back stiffened. "It's no worse than the hot dog smell we've had to live with since you moved in," she lashed back.

"You and your bean sprouts and prune yogurt. I saw you sneaking in last night after the store was closed. Don't think I can't put two and two together." He spat on the sidewalk. "I can't even talk to you. I'll let my lawyers do it." And he walked away, red-faced and muttering.

"Corso," Dad called after him, "we are genuinely sorry about your shop." But Mr. Corso didn't turn back.

"How are you guys doing?" Dad asked, turning to Aaron and Lenny. "You come to see the towering inferno?" We were embarrassed about the fight, all of us—except maybe Mom, who just seemed mad. I stuck the toe of my shoe in the puddle of fire water that had formed in the gutter. It had been there so long that ice was beginning to harden around its edges.

"Don't worry about him," Dad told us, looking after Mr. Corso. "Of course he's upset. How's your tooth, tiger?" he asked Aaron, and Aaron raised his upper lip, chipmunk-like, to show it off. What a weird tooth. "Sarah, would you look at this!" He pulled her over with a hug.

She looked in Aaron's mouth and shook her head weakly. "I bet your dad's proud of it," she said.

"Yes, ma'am," Aaron said. "Me, too."

"We heard the sirens just after school started today," Lenny told them, "while we were eating Mitch's famous Health Nutty Gingerbread."

"Oh, good grief," Mom sighed. "I'd completely forgotten about Miami Beach and the gingerbread. That's supposed to be tomorrow, isn't it? I feel so woozy, I don't know if I can make it, and your dad's going to meet with the arson people. Is your heart set on it, honey? Oh, Mitch," she said weakly, wiping at her forehead with the back of her hand, "can we possibly go?" Dad eased her down on the curb and she put her head on her knees.

I'd forgotten about it, too, like I couldn't think of more than one thing at a time. And it seems funny but I didn't see how we could go either. It was like the store had died or something and it wouldn't be right to just leave it there alone.

The police had driven their cars away and traffic was moving again. It was slow, though, because people were stopping to stare.

Mom raised her head and began to cry. It wasn't the kind of crying from the chest that you see kids do. Tears were just coming out of her eyes as she looked at something across the street. Then, she gave a hiccup-like laugh that didn't go with the tears at all.

"Lenny, you'll like this," she said. "Look what happened to our sign." And she pointed. The plastic sign above the awning had oozed down out of its metal frame. The letter "S" had completely melted away, so that in squishly, freaky letters it now read, "UN-SHINE."

"That's the advice we're left with, folks—Un-shine. Isn't that funny, Lenny?" she said with a weird laugh.

"No, Mrs. McDandel," Lenny said, looking over at the mess. "It isn't funny at all."

7

Megabucks for the McDandels

SLEEP CAME EASY THE NIGHT OF THE FIRE. I THOUGHT sirens would circle in my head, signs would melt, and peanut butter machines char, but I just closed my eyes and that was that. It was still dark, though, when I woke. Mom was shaking my shoulder.

"Mitch! Mitch! Wake up, baby. Mitch, I've got to talk to you."

"Mom? What time is it?" The light wasn't on. I could hardly see her face. "Is something wrong?"

She laughed the same unfunny way she'd laughed at the sign the day before. "No. Nothing's wrong. Nothing more than yesterday anyway. We can't top that right away."

"What time is it? Is it time to get up?" It felt like the middle of the night.

"It's early. Five-thirty."

"Why is it five-thirty?"

"Because time marches relentlessly on. Mitch, listen to me. I've decided we're going to Florida today after all. The tickets are free, and I don't have to worry about working at the store this afternoon." She laughed again. "Besides, I've already spent some of the one hundred dollars they sent for expense money."

"Are you sure?" I asked. "Are you sure you feel like it?"

"Absolutely. My head was filled with smoke last night, but now I can think clear and I've decided it's just what we need. I've been figuring out the whole situation . . . and I've decided . . ." She seemed to forget what she was saying. She didn't finish the sentence.

"How long have you been awake?"

"I didn't go to sleep. I couldn't. Your father has been zonked out for hours. He was tired, I guess. But I just . . . couldn't . . ." She faded off again. Then she looked at me and her eyes brightened, and she really smiled. "Mitch, that contest of yours . . . I'd always thought of that contest as being a kind of diverting game for you, nothing serious. It didn't really occur to me you might win. Most people aren't all that big on natural foods. You come to accept that. I just thought of it as one of your crazy contests. But all at once . . . around three o'clock, I think . . . I knew it was the answer. What we need right now more than anything else is something grand like thirty thousand dollars in the bank. If only I had . . . There are things I want to *do*. You know, start out fresh."

She reached over and turned on the lamp by my bed. "And you can get it as easy as pie." I blinked against the light. Her shoulders shook as she laughed. "As easy as gingerbread."

I was wide awake by then, five-thirty or not. "You said my gingerbread isn't the kind of thing that wins big money," I told her. "And yesterday in class when I let the kids try some, I might as well have been feeding them sweat socks."

"No, no, I've thought about that." She started walking up and down in my room, leaning over occasionally to pick up a sock or a book from the floor. "That's exactly what I've been thinking about. That's what I've been doing since three o'clock—or three-thirty— I've been making it possible for you to *win* this contest. I've been changing your recipe to make it what Lenny would call 'brain-rotting' good."

"You've changed it?" It was almost too much to believe, but she seemed so excited and pleased. "My recipe?"

"Listen to this, we'll beat them at their own game. It's beautiful. I've put in a half-cup of granulated sugar, taken out the carrots, and written an icing recipe with bales of confectioners' sugar in it. As soon as you bite into it you'll taste both sugar and spice. Sugar and Spicebread, that's not a bad name. You think it's too late to change the name?"

"I think it's too late to change it, period."

"I thought for a while you could get up and practice making it now," she went on, without listening to what I said, "but I don't have any sugar and I think it's still too early to knock on a neighbor's door and ask to borrow a cup." Her voice was high and loud for the nighttime. "There used to be all-night grocery stores, lots of them, but I don't know where they've all gone. I don't think even the 7-Eleven opens now until seven. The precious supermarket doesn't open till eight. So why don't you just get up and pack. I haven't packed yet either." She massaged her forehead with her fingertips.

"You feel OK?" I asked her.

"I feel fabulous," she said, grinning. "My incredible son and I are off to the fabled southland to make megabucks for the needy McDandels. Tons of money. And I haven't even packed. I wonder if your camera burned in the fire? Where is it, do you know?"

"Mom, why don't you get some sleep?"

"Because the plane leaves at nine-thirty, and there's a lot to do before then. Look in the closet for the suitcases, will you? No, I think we only have one in operating order. It's been so long since we've had a vacation. You can pack your things in your hockey duffle. That's way big enough."

While she put some clothes in the washer, I found a short-sleeved, button-down yellow dress shirt and a few other things I thought I might need. A lot of last summer's stuff looked small for me and scruffy from wear, but I packed all I thought I would wear on a Saturday, Sunday, and Monday in a warm place. After gathering up all the papers the Bakeathon people had sent me, I decided I'd covered everything.

"Do you have a swimsuit?" I asked Mom. It was six-fifteen.

"I've got a two-piece job that's five years old," she said. "But it still fits. If only I can find it." She'd been tiptoeing in and out of the bedroom to keep from waking Dad, but the swimsuit search finally did it.

"What *time* is it?" Dad asked, his voice hoarse. "It's still dark outside."

"We're packing," Mom said. Then she whispered to me very urgently, "Don't tell him about the recipe. He wouldn't understand." I didn't understand, either, but that didn't seem to bother her.

"I thought you weren't going. After yesterday." He yawned.

"Well, we are," she said cheerfully. "Want to come along?"

"I can't afford it," he said. "They only sent two tickets. You sure you're up to it? Couldn't Mitch go by himself?"

"He's just a baby. Of course not. No, I'll lie in the sun for three days," she said. "Unless you need me here. Do you think you'll need me here for anything?"

"Sure, I need you," he said, "but I can take care of

things for a few days if this is what you want to do."

"It's Mitch's contest," she said, "and I wouldn't want to disappoint him. It's not *his* fault we had a fire. He'll have a wonderful time. And," she said lightly, "he might even win."

So Dad stayed up and fixed us a big breakfast as we packed. Mom didn't eat any, though. By eight o'clock we were ready for Dad to drive us over to catch the airport bus. Mom was wearing my camera. "Pictures for posterity!" she said. Then she turned back to Dad and said, "They won't think I'm skipping out of town, will they?"

It took us both a minute to figure she meant the police. "Out!" Dad said, swatting her forward with the suitcase. "You're a crazy today," he said, smiling. "What you need is a weekend in the sun."

It was a cold, calm day. The little bit of snow still on the ground from the last falling was all frozen together and crusty with dirt and ice. You couldn't make a decent snowball from it. Mom and Dad and me stood inside the Barrington Hotel waiting for the airport bus to pick us up. Mom said she and Dad would keep an eye out, so I climbed up and down the little winding staircase that led to the second floor where a sign said "Banquet Rooms." There were no risers on the steps and underneath you could see a fountain and pool with lots of rocks beside it so it looked like the country. There were goldfish in the pool, big, fat ones.

Also there were cigarette butts and pennies and gum wrappers, not exactly goldfish health food, but they couldn't be choosy. They couldn't swim over the dam to another goldfish pond. I was just climbing back down the steps to the grassy carpet when Dad yelled that the bus had come.

What I wanted to do was get back in the car and go home. And go to bed. And hide my head under the covers. I had the old recipe packed in my duffle. Mom had the new one tucked carefully in her purse. When she'd put it in she'd winked at me like we shared some great secret. The driver had tossed our bags into a luggage holder and Dad had already kissed Mom goodbye. He turned to me. "Well," he said, laying his hands on my shoulders, "wave the good natural food banner, Mitch. Don't scrape your fingers with the carrot grater, and have a fantastic time." Leaning over, he whispered in my ear, "Take care your mother gets some rest."

I climbed on board after Mom and settled back into the window seat next to her. We waved goodbye out the window. Just in case the bus went past Sunshine, I closed my eyes and pretended to sleep. The velvety seats were comfortable and I almost didn't have to pretend.

When I opened my eyes we were driving through a place I'd never seen before. The bus had stopped at a light and on the corner was the Look of Love

Doggie Boutique. There were frilly yellow curtains over the windows so I couldn't tell if it was a fancy pet store or a dog beauty shop. What a lot of nutty stores there are in this world, I thought. Is there always room for one more?

We pulled up to another hotel to take on passengers, and the man and woman who got on sat behind us. Hearing their conversation was like listening to the radio, except I'd like to have turned up the volume. He was going to Las Vegas to judge a *cat* contest. They were talking about chocolate and blue cats and Himalayas and seal points and one-day shows and two-day shows. I asked Mom if she was listening, but she said good grief, no, and it wasn't any of my business what they were saying back there. But still I listened. The only cats I knew were nervous as cats and wouldn't stand still for anybody to pet them, let alone judge them. I wondered if cats knew when they got blue ribbons for being beautiful? And if they cared.

I'd been to the airport before when we'd picked people up or dropped them off, but I'd never been on a plane myself. Mom had, but not me. As we got off the bus, I wished again that I wasn't going. I mean, you read about airplanes crashing and killing everybody. A kid in my school—he was in the same Scout troop as Aaron—he was going to California to visit his grandparents. He'd promised to bring Aaron back one of those Mickey Mouse-ears caps from Disneyland, only his plane crashed when it was taking off from Chicago and he never got there. We looked at the pictures of it on TV and wondered where he was sitting and what he was thinking the minute it took for the crash to happen.

Inside the airport nobody looked scared. There were millions of people. Some of them had skis and backpacks. Standing in the check-in line next to ours was a kid holding a pink-nosed white rabbit in a cage. He was calling it Roger and trying to calm it down. I wondered if they were going to a pink-nosed white-rabbit contest and if Roger would win. I tried to listen and find out, but Mom had already given the check-in man our bags and was tugging me toward our gate.

Along the way we passed a big bunch of tan people with necklaces of flowers. Mom said they were coming home from Hawaii. I never knew so many people went so many places so early on a Saturday morning.

Next we got in line to be funneled through a booth that was supposed to ring bells if it caught us carrying bombs or machine guns. Mom didn't want to walk through it, and wouldn't, until they told her it didn't X-ray her like she thought it did. The X-ray machine just took pictures of her purse as it traveled along on a moving belt. It was neat. All those gray shadows on the X-ray screen looked like things the purse had eaten for breakfast. Mom refused to let them X-ray the camera because, she said, it would ruin the pictures in it we took last summer. The warning bell actually rang for the man behind me. He looked like a normal guy in a gray suit, but Mom wouldn't let me wait around to see if he was a killer.

"Look at that," Mom hissed, jabbing me in the side. It was a snack place that smelled like Mr. Corso's store. "Those crazy people are standing in line at nine in the morning to buy steamed *hot dogs*! Can you believe it?"

I couldn't. The smell made me woozy.

"Are you hungry?" she asked me. "I've got apples and tangerines in my purse. You don't suppose the X-rays hurt them, do you?"

A plane was taxiing in and I wanted to see, so we walked into a United Airlines waiting room to watch. Out on the field a guy wearing big earmuffs was showing the plane exactly where to park. Just as a tunnel that looked like an accordion was opening out to the plane door, Mom pulled me away. "We don't want to be late," she said. "Planes don't wait, and we've got too much at stake to miss that flight."

Just like Marie's bus, I thought, except I bet they don't say, "Move it!"

I'd like to work out here, I thought. There's so much happening. Little trains of luggage cars were snaking around between the planes. We stopped just for a second at the next gate to watch men throw suitcases onto a belt that fed them into the plane's belly. Is that where the white rabbit will ride? I wondered. Will he sit down there looking at red and blue and plaid suitcases, wondering where his buddy is who calls him Roger?

I looked up to ask Mom where they put rabbits on airplanes, but I couldn't see her anywhere. The corridors were at a crossroads, with one going off to the right and another to the left. I didn't see her either way. She had disappeared. A kid passed me, wearing a blue sweatband on his head with red satin horns sticking out of it. Ordinarily I would have smiled at him to let him know I liked the horns, but I couldn't. All I could think of was that he was with his mom and I wasn't. I turned around and started running back to where it said, "To Terminal," until I saw a guy in a uniform. Maybe he was a pilot.

"Excuse me, sir," I said. "I don't . . . I can't . . . I . . ."

"What's wrong, kid?" I must have looked crazy scared, because I was.

"I can't find my mom," I said with a catch in my throat like I was a baby lost in a department store. "She was just here. She's got to be here somewhere. We're going to Miami Beach," I told him. "She's short and has red hair like mine and she's wearing blue corduroy jeans and a yellow quilted vest thing—"

"OK, OK," he said calmly. "Now, what's your name?"

"Mitchell McDandel, 449 Fullerton Street—"

"Hold up. No need for rank and serial number." He smiled like he thought I was funny.

Out the window I saw a plane pull away from its gate. What if it was mine? I started to dash off again but he grabbed me. "Let's try paging," he said. He picked up the receiver from a yellow phone on the wall and asked me my mom's name.

"Sarah McDandel," I told him, "from Evanston, Illinois." He said something into the phone and pretty soon I heard over the loudspeaker, "Sandra McDaniel. Mrs. Sandra McDaniel. Please meet your party at Gate C-4, United Airlines." I looked up at the sign and that's where I was standing. Would she realize that name was her? I started to ask the man to try again with the right name, but he smiled down kindly and said, "Not to worry." I worried anyway, searching the hall both ways.

I bet it wasn't really more than a minute, though, before I saw Mom almost flying down the hall, dodging whole families of people who were hurrying in the opposite direction. I ran to meet her.

"Where *were* you?" she said, grabbing me by the hand. "I *told* you while you were standing there watching that plane that I was going to the washroom. I *know* I did. Good grief, I feel like I've aged ten years. I couldn't imagine what had happened."

"I'm sorry," I told her. "I didn't hear . . . I thought I was lost. I asked this man . . . this pilot . . ." I turned to look for him but he was gone in the crowd. I never did get to thank him.

In the plane, though, we were lucky. I mean, we sat together, me by a window. There were those people I really felt sorry for who had to sit five to a row in the middle of the plane and couldn't even see out a window.

Somehow, I'd never really wondered before how planes stayed up in the air. They just did. But as I looked around and saw how many people were in that plane for rows and rows in front of me and behind me, I realized that it didn't make any sense that something so heavy should go up in the air, let alone stay there. A man whose stomach bulged out over his belt walked past. If he sat next to a window, would that make the plane tilt?

Mom was reading a plastic instruction sheet she'd taken from the pocket of the seat in front of her. When I looked to see if she was scared, too, she said, "Fasten your seat belt."

As the plane moved backward to the runway a baby started to cry. It was far enough away not to drown out the stewardess up front who was telling us how to use oxygen masks and how to escape and what to do if we crashed in water. *She* didn't expect the plane to fly either.

Rummaging through her purse, Mom found a piece of sugarless gum for me and I let go of the armrests I had been clutching long enough to unwrap it and pop it into my mouth. When we started to move forward, I could feel the power in the plane. Flaps on the wing outside my window lowered. Were they supposed to do that? I felt like Orville Wright. I was going to have to make that plane stay up all by myself. The little flaps kept moving and I half expected the whole wing to beat up and down like a bird's.

The pilot came on the loudspeaker and told us we could listen to the tower on our headsets, so I let go again long enough to put them on and turn to Channel 9. There was a lot of static, then ". . . 496 . . . maintain flight level . . . tower . . . code Good Day . . . 210 . . . 270 Happy 33. . . . Delta 547 make a right turn then hold short of 22. . . . We're looking to see if we can make it here. . . . Delta 547, please continue as planned."

We must have been Delta 547 because we were continuing faster and faster. The wing quivered. The wheels were still on the ground, so maybe it wasn't too late to stop.

Even with my eyes closed, I could tell when the plane went up. When I opened them just a second later the expressway below already was so small it looked like it was filled with Hot Wheels. A cloud flashed past my window and suddenly there was nothing outside but cloud gray and then, just as suddenly, white pillows of clouds below us and pure blue sky above.

"Mom?" I asked. "Were you scared?"

"Yes," she said. "But I bet you weren't." She grinned, and I thought, Why, she's been nervous, that's why she's been like that. Now everything's going to be all right. In a few minutes we'll be laughing about her even considering changing my recipe to Sugar and Spicebread.

The loudspeaker crackled on and we could hear the captain again. "This is Captain Webner," he said, with a reassuring smile in his voice. "We'll be cruising down to Miami Beach at thirty-seven thousand feet, flying right over Music City, passing west of Atlanta, and along the western shore of Florida. The latest weather in Miami Beach is scattered clouds with a temperature of eighty degrees. Flying time will be two hours and twenty minutes. Enjoy your flight."

Pretty soon they gave us a menu, and even though Mom was suspicious with her apples and tangerines out just in case, she let me get the Baked Chicken Biscayne: "Orange sauce and toasted coconut top a boneless chicken leg, which has been baked until golden brown. Served with rice and green beans with water chestnuts." I ate mine. She picked at hers. The

Orange Sunburst Cake was pure sugar, so we ate our tangerines for dessert.

"You were kidding," I said, "about turning my gingerbread into a sweet cake. That was kind of a joke, wasn't it?" She turned her head away and said nothing at all.

Outside and down I could see a river snaking its way in big S's across the earth. We seemed so far away. And the moon was up above. Why, at thirty-seven thousand feet up, didn't it look any bigger?

"On your left is Atlanta," the captain announced before too long. I looked down and saw that the earth was red in Atlanta. People I can't see are running races down there, I thought, with red dirt under their toenails.

Mom was very quiet, shuffling through a magazine. I dozed off, my head on a little pillow with a paper pillowcase the stewardess had given me. Fortunately, she'd passed me by when she was handing out those junior pilot pins. She must have realized I was beyond all that.

"Ladies and gentlemen, we're preparing for landing at Miami International Airport," I heard as I woke. "Please raise your seats and tray tables to an upright position and make certain your seat belts are securely fastened." We were going down. And I had only just gotten used to the idea of being up. I didn't feel good. A lump was rising in my throat. Should I reach for that little white paper bag marked "In case of motion discomfort?"

"Mom," I said, my voice shaking, "how do you get to be a pilot? I mean is it doggy-dog? Do only the best ones make it?"

"I don't know," she said, without smiling. "But I sure hope so."

Out the window I could see swimming pools in people's backyards. And palm trees. They got bigger and bigger. The plane bumped lightly on the ground. We were in Florida.

8

The Royal Imperial Towers Hotel

"GOOD GRIEF, THIS PLACE IS GARISH," MOM SAID, LOOKING over the lobby of the Royal Imperial Towers hotel. It was the most beautiful place I'd ever seen. Way up on the high, high ceilings were chandeliers as big as bathtubs—bigger even. In the broad daylight they were turned on, their crystal beads glittering. The wallpaper was red-purple with flowers on it that felt like velvet, the lobby pillars were covered with thick orange-and-red-pile carpeting, and, at the bottom of a wide marble staircase, little gold cupid statues were playing harps. It was heaven.

While Mom got us checked into the hotel I guarded our bags and held on to my jacket and her yellow vest. We'd both rolled our long sleeves up. Even inside it was plenty warm. Boy, did that happen fast, two-and-a-half hours from snow to sweat.

Mom gave the guy who carried our bags to our room a dollar bill. The room was fabulous, just like the lobby. Gold lamps with red-and-black shades, mirrors with little silver patterns around the edges, and a huge bathroom with an orange sunlamp in the ceiling you could turn on if you wanted to get a tan while you sat on the john. I liked Florida very much.

While I was turning knobs and looking in drawers and reading the room-service menu, Mom lay down on her bed and asked me please to close the drapes. It seemed a shame since when they were open you could see the ocean. It looked big and blue and frothy, not a whole lot different from Lake Michigan in the summer.

"Mitch," she said, "I'm sorry, but I've got a crazy, wild, awful headache. I don't know whether it's the fire or the food or no sleep or the heat or what, but I'm going to lie down awhile. Why don't you go register at the contest desk to let them know you're here. There are probably things they want you to do. Make sure you do everything right, OK?"

I pulled the drapes. They had a thick silver liner that cut out all the light from the bright day. I was glad she was going to rest like Dad had said.

"Take the key and keep it in your right-hand pocket so you'll remember where it is, and Mitch . . . Mitch, look in my purse for the new recipe. Don't worry about our changing it. It's the only way it can win. I've thought the whole thing out. I want you to memorize the way the new one goes. Maybe sugar isn't all that bad. Like the woman said, her mother lived to be ninety on chocolate cake." She curled up on the bed, her back toward me.

It didn't seem like the time to argue. I found the recipe like she said, stuffed it into my pocket, took the key, and let myself softly out the door. She was still counting on me and Sugar and Spicebread. She still expected us to win thirty thousand dollars. I wasn't so sure anymore.

I had to go down two long halls to get to the elevator, but at least I didn't have to remember where it was. A long silver arrow on the wall pointed the way. Inside the elevator there were three women wearing orange-and-white badges shaped like birthday cakes. "Tenth ABC Bakeathon" was printed over the candles and their names and hometowns were written underneath in calligraphy.

The lady at the Hospitality Desk really knocked me out. I mean, I just sort of expected to sign my name and get a list of things to do, but she said, "So, you're Mitchell McDandel! We are very glad to see you. I've tried your recipe and I like it."

"You're kidding," I said, feeling in my pocket for Mom's new version. "How did you do that?"

"Easy. I'm one of the ABC home economists. I baked the Health Nutty Gingerbread you saw photographed over there." I must have looked blank because she said, "Didn't you see the picture of it?" I hadn't. So she just pinned a Mitchell McDandel fancy cake-shaped badge on me, and told me to come back for my folder later, but meanwhile, just to march right over and look.

I ran over to where she pointed. There were a bunch of bulletin boards with pictures of food on each side, eight-by-ten glossy photos, in color. One or two people with badges were looking, saying which was theirs and which ones they thought looked best. A gray-haired lady from Independence, Missouri, who told me she'd made her Coconut Crown Peanut Pie using icing mix, showed me its picture. Then she helped me find mine in the bread division. She said the recipes were made in a test kitchen and that each one was photographed by a professional photographer. I could believe it, too. My gingerbread had never looked that good at home. The picture had it sitting in a wicker basket lined with a green-and-white-checked napkin. A thick slice was set out on a white plate with a green border and little crumbs were sprinkled on the plate, the kind of crumbs you want pick up on your finger and taste. A big frothy glass of milk in the background looked icy cold. Did my gingerbread really look that good? I wondered if they'd cheated.

"That looks absolutely scrumptious," the Coconut Crown Peanut Pie lady said and moved on down to look at the Zucchini Bread Supreme.

I thought for sure mine was the best until I started looking close at the others. They were all straight out of magazine ads.

"Let's go. Can't we just *go* now?" a kid on the other side of the bulletin board said impatiently.

"Now, Willie Ruth, honey, don't you go get nervous and high strung. You know how to bake it and you've practiced over and over what you're going to say to all those reporters who'll ask you questions tomorrow."

"Stop bugging me," the kid said. "I know all that. I'd just rather be home at Marlene's party than here with your crazy recipe."

"It's a *darling* recipe. And it's *your* recipe, not *my* recipe. You just put that out of your head and let me hear it proper one more time."

After a sigh and a long pause, the kid put on a baby voice and started her speech. Since she was on the other side of the bulletin board I couldn't see her, but she sounded obnoxious. The kid was wearing yellow sandals. Her mother's shoes were blue with lions on the buckles. I moved back so they couldn't see my feet.

"My mamma," she whined, "taught me to cook when I was practically a *baby*. I make all the good old traditional middle-Tennessee *favorites*. I make sausage biscuits, and chicken 'n dumplings, and peach fried pies, and jam cake. My mamma was one of the *finalists* in this contest five years ago with *her* version of the jam cake using plum preserves. She called it Plum Perfection Jam Cake. Since she can't win again because she's won before and is *in-eligible*, she *urged* me to enter my very *own* version of an old English favorite my great-great-great grandmother brought over from Chichester."

"Chichester, England," her mother corrected her.

"I said old *English* favorite. OK . . . OK . . . old *English* favorite that my great-great-great-great-*great* grandmother brought over from Chichester, *England.* Will that do?"

"That sounds just fine, Willie Ruth, if you don't say it so snippy and if you make it sound more natural, not so much like it's memorized."

"It *is* memorized," the kid said. "Look, so long as I'm in Florida, I'm going to sit in the sun."

"You sure the sun won't tire you out, now? Tomorrow's going to be your big day, Willie Ruth."

"Oh, Mamma, it may be your idea of a big day to stand around and cook with a lot of old ladies, but it sure isn't mine. I'm going to put on my swimsuit and sit on the beach. You stay here and talk to people about recipes for corn pone. I'll see you around six."

"You know good and well that orientation meeting's at five. You be there at five o'clock sharp, hear? And dressed like a lady." The feet on the other side of the bulletin board stalked off in opposite directions. I waited until I was sure they had gone, walked around to the opposite side, and searched the pictures until I found one by Willie Ruth Jennings, Murfreesboro, Tennessee. It was called Toad in the Hole. No kidding.

I told the home economist at Hospitality that I liked the picture of my gingerbread and what a good job she did baking it. She told me about the orientation and about dinner. "You must wear your badge at all times. It's your ticket into places," she said. "Here's one for your mother, too." She looked around, trying to locate her.

"She's taking a nap," I said.

"Oh, yes, the heat affected me like that, too. I came down from Milwaukee day before yesterday and could hardly keep my eyes open all day. Well, then, here's a map of the hotel that shows where the pool is, and the game rooms in case it rains. You'll do just fine by yourself for an hour or two. If you need anything, just stop by."

The folders, maps, and stuff might cheer up Mom, I thought. I could hardly wait to watch her laugh when I told her about Willie Ruth Jennings. I'd only gotten a few steps away from the desk, though, before I spotted that same pair of blue shoes with lion buckles I'd seen just minutes before. Willie Ruth's mother. She was shaped like a dumpling, no sharp angles at all. Pumping the hands of another lady, she was saying, "Well, I guess I had my place in the sun. Now my baby is going to be out there on the floor tomorrow baking her heart out." I turned back to the Hospitality Desk.

"Excuse me, Ms. Stern," I said, reading her name off her badge. "Can you tell me if there are many other kids in this contest?"

"Just one," she said. "A darling little girl from Tennessee."

When I got back upstairs I found Mom sitting on the balcony outside our room in her swimsuit. She said her head still hurt but since she couldn't sleep she might as well get some sun. When I told her about Willie Ruth and about the great color picture of my gingerbread without icing, she seeemed to be thinking about something else. "Why don't you go outside and play in the sand," she said like I was in nursery school.

I thought maybe I could make her see how funny it sounded. "Because I forgot my pail and shovel," I told her.

She reached down, picked up the purse beside her, and pulled out a five-dollar bill. "They must sell them downstairs," she said mechanically.

"You need anything from the drugstore?" I asked her.

"Oh, no, no," she smiled and then looked out at the ocean. "I'll be all right. My headache will be gone by tonight. There's a dinner tonight, don't I remember that? I promise to be well by then."

My swimsuit was gray-green, faded from last summer and almost a size too small. I put it on with an orange T-shirt that said "Sunshine Natural Foods," a pair of sneakers without socks, and, to hide under, the new Cubs cap Dad had bought me at the end of last season. Right up on the shoulder above Sunshine I pinned the Mitchell McDandel, Evanston, Illinois, Bakeathon badge and looked at it in reverse in the mirror.

"There's an orientation at five o'clock, so I'll see you here before that," I said. She didn't answer. If she's not better by tonight, I thought, I'll call Dad. I stuck the key and the five-dollar bill in my shoe.

As I walked through the halls, I saw a long black streak on the beautiful fuzzy, flowered wallpaper. I don't know why but it made me think about Sunshine, and about the snow at home covered with dirt. Dad had told me to take care that Mom got rested, but I'd never had to take care of my mom before. She always told *me* what to do. But she'd been so down lately—even before the fire—that I couldn't help but wonder . . .

Everything is going to be all right though, I thought, as the elevator door opened in front of me. That's what everybody said, so it must be true. Inside the elevator badgeless people stared at me, and I could feel my face turn red. If I didn't have this sign on, I decided, they wouldn't even see me.

I checked the map I'd brought and followed it, turn for turn, down to a shopping floor called the Lower Lobby, past a cocktail lounge named the Brown Teddy Bear, a kid's clothing shop with neat shirts in the window that had tiny flashing traffic lights on their pockets, and then to a drugstore where I didn't buy a plastic pail. I did buy a newspaper to check my horoscope: "Improve relations with friends by having serious talks about important subjects. Control your temper." Carefully I tore it out and tucked it in my shoe with the key and the change. I glanced at the comics, shuffled through the sports section, and threw the rest of the paper away.

When I finally got outside to the swimming pool I just stood there and stared. It was the most incredible pool I've ever seen, huge and round, sitting just a few yards back from the ocean. The Y pool at home wasn't even its poor cousin. What was really wild, though, was that smack in the middle was an island planted with real palm trees. On the island was a mountain two stories high built of craggy fake rocks with waterfalls shooting out of them. I thought of the dinky little fountain under the stairs at the Barrington Hotel at home. Those goldfish would have been wild about Florida, too.

A lot more people were stretched out on chairs by

the pool than were swimming in it. A plump woman in a bright green swimsuit was sitting up in her deck chair reading cookbooks, a stack of them beside her like she was studying for a test. But rows of bodies were just lying there all tan and glossy, like their colors had been painted on. The air smelled sweet and thick of coconut suntan oil mixed with a slightly fishy ocean.

A bunch of kids climbing around on the mountain island kept disappearing inside it, so I threw my shirt and sneakers on an empty chair, tossed my cap next to them, and jumped in the water to investigate. I nearly croaked. No wonder people were sitting around the pool instead of doing laps in it. It was filled with salt water that stung where you'd just scratched and tasted like tears. I grabbed on to the edge and wondered if they'd got that awful salty water from the ocean, and if so, why. Once I was used to the taste and weird stickiness, I swam over to the island to see what the kids were doing. I wasn't disappointed either. Following the line of them, I climbed up a green-lit spiral staircase inside the fake mountain until I came to a slide that cut through the phony rocks like a slalom course. It was cool. The slide shot you into the other side of the salty pool straight through a salty waterfall.

I'd whirled my way around about ten times, feeling

good and dizzy and briney like a pickle, when I heard a voice behind me say, "My mamma is going to be plenty mad when she sees my hair. She paid twenty-five dollars for me to get it set yesterday and when she sees it soaked and stringy like this she'll die." That voice couldn't belong to anybody but Willie Ruth Jennings. I turned around to see what she looked like.

She smiled when I turned. She'd been talking to me. "It's all right with me, though," she went on. "I prefer it straight. What I wish it was, though, is short. But Mamma says no."

While she may have sounded like a whiney, smart-mouth brat, Willie Ruth Jennings was really something. She looked like fifteen. Her skin was pale as winter, like it had never seen a tan. She had huge violet eyes with blue stuff on the eyelids, long wet black hair, and an excellent smile. She was wearing a shiny silver two-piece suit made out of the crackled metallic stuff astronauts wear in space. It had to be brand new. And it fit her.

I smiled at her. You couldn't help smiling at her.

"You look all pasty like I do," she said. "You just get here, too?" I kept smiling. One of her eyes had gold flecks in it. "Say, you're not here for the contest, are you?" she went on.

"Yeah," I said, "I am. My mom and me got here an hour or so ago."

"Will you guys move it!" a little kid with a peeling nose yelled. "If you've gotta talk, talk someplace else. I wanna slide."

I slid round and round into the water and Willie Ruth flew out of the waterfall so close behind me her feet grazed my shoulder. She swam to a rock on the side of the island and I dog-paddled after, keeping my eyes on her.

"Well, this *is* something," she said. "I thought I'd be the only one here under forty."

"I'm twelve—going on thirteen," I told her.

"Oh, well, you're tall. I'm fourteen, almost fifteen. I'm a freshman at Oakland High School, and I'm missing Marlene Hahn's Sweet Sixteen party tonight. I was supposed to go with Gardiner Winslow. Have you ever been to a Sweet Sixteen party?"

"I don't know a whole lot of people who are sixteen," I told her, wishing I could think of something exciting to say. She wasn't going to sit there talking to me long unless I did. Already she was looking off toward the other side of the pool where two guys had picked up this extremely tan, bikinied girl and were about to toss her into the water.

"What's your sign—sign of the zodiac?" I tried.

"Leo, I think," she said. "It means I'm aggressive."

The kid with the peeling nose swam by and Willie Ruth kicked the water absently. The splash got him right in the face.

"I guess your mom got you to come down here because of the warm weather?" she asked, watching the girl wriggle free from her tossers.

I had to tell her something that would really get her attention, get her to look at me, at least. "We almost didn't come," I said, swimming around to the other side of her and grabbing on to the rock ledge. "Yesterday at home we had a tragedy." She turned to me, her eyes very big. I don't know why, but people like hearing about tragedies. I'd watched it happen as people talked to Mom and Dad about the fire. "It was awful," I went on slow. "We heard the sirens from the fire engines at school, hundreds of sirens, but I didn't know what they were for until Leroi Rupert—he's this very famous disc jockey back home— he got me out of school and told me I had to come with him because my parents' store had burned down."

"You're not puttin' me on?" she asked, touching me on the shoulder. Goose bumps grew down my arm and up to my ear. "Just yesterday? Did it burn all the way to the ground?"

"No, it was gutted, though," I said, describing it the way Dad did to somebody on the phone. While I knew it was crummy of me to be using the fire like that, I couldn't help it. I tried to think of some grimy details to make her see how awful it was, how sorry she should feel. "It's a really terrible tragedy," I went on, watching her jaw hang loose as she stared at me.

"*All* our money was tied up in the store. And the *worst* of it is," I said, knowing I'd get her with this, "the guy who owns the place next door and the police both think my folks set the fire. That's arson, you know, and it's a crime and you have to go to jail for it."

"What's your name?" she asked me, really interested now in who I was. She put her hand on mine and squeezed it. "Where you from, anyway? Somewhere up North?"

I swallowed the lump in my throat, told her, and then realized she didn't know I knew who *she* was. So I asked her.

She told me, drawing her name out long, like she liked the sound of it. "I'm named after my daddy, William Jennings. He raises Tennessee walking horses. I own ten of them all by myself. It's for tax purposes, Daddy says, but no matter what purposes they're mine. I'd hate it if the stables burned." She cocked her head and started chewing on her little finger. "Somebody in my class has a daddy who's in prison," she went on suddenly. "This boy I know only a little. His daddy tried to rob a savings and loan over at Smyrna, but they caught him at it."

"Oh, I didn't mean my folks *did* it," I told her. "They wouldn't actually do a thing like burning down their own store. It's just that this guy and the police *think* they did."

"Look *I* didn't say they burned it. You don't need

to be so snippy. Did they need the money, though? Sometimes people go stark raving wild when they're desperate for money, and they do things you don't think anybody could do. My friend's daddy, when he was out on bail, he got in his car and started off to Memphis at ninety miles an hour, but the police stopped him. And the judge said he was guilty and had to go to jail." She looked at me closely and frowned. "What would you do if your mamma and daddy went to jail?"

"They didn't do anything," I told her. "I said they *didn't* do it." As fast as I could I got out of that water, hunted down my shirt and shoes, and rushed away without looking back. Who did she think she was, saying things like that? My folks hadn't done anything wrong. Had they?

9

I, the Undersigned

WHEN I WENT UP TO GET DRESSED FOR THE ORIENTATION meeting, Mom was zonked out, snoring loud asleep. So I quick changed out of my salt-wet suit, took a shower, baked for a minute under the sunlamp, and then put on jeans and a red plaid shirt. As I grabbed my badge I knocked over an empty glass on the dresser and Mom started making soft, crying sounds.

"You awake?" I whispered.

Nothing. And then a little hiccupping snore.

On the table next to the bed was a pad of Royal Imperial Towers hotel notepaper, so I wrote Mom a note telling her I'd be back in time for dinner, and once more let myself quietly out the door.

After I'd listened to the lock click, I wished I'd called Dad. But what would I have said? That Mom was finally sleeping? That I'd heard the firemen say that maybe he and Mom had started the fire? That I was having a wonderful time and wished he was here?

None of the above. Besides, I thought, staring down at the key in my hand, a call like that would probably cost a bundle, and we didn't have a bundle.

Downstairs I tried to store all that in the back of my brain, and there was so much going on that it wasn't all that hard. The orientation meeting was behind a big arched white door marked in gold letters "Crystal Ballroom." A uniformed guy with a walkie-talkie stood in front of it. In his belt where you'd expect to see a gun he had a flashlight. If somebody tried to force his way in, I wondered if the guard would draw his flashlight on them. He glanced down at my badge and opened the door for me, so I didn't find out.

The ballroom was as incredible as the swimming pool, big enough to play three basketball games in at one time. But it didn't look like a gym. The satiny gold wallpaper glowed behind fancy candle-like lights. Tons of chandeliers dripped with crystal beads. The chandeliers looked twice as big as they really were, too, because they were reflected in mirrors on the ceiling. But the floor of the ballroom was even wilder than the mirrored ceiling because on it there were one hundred stoves lined up in ten rows, ten stoves to a row. Next to each stove was a cooking counter. One hundred tiny kitchens in one glittery room, like it was for Cinderella in her ball gown *and* apron.

I edged over to a cluster of people where the Coconut Crown Peanut Pie woman was talking to a lady in a big flowered hat.

"My husband is so tired of my Hot Dilly Dog Buns I may never make them again after tomorrow. Every night at home for two weeks we've had them for supper just to make sure I'll do it perfect tomorrow. We sure could use the money," the hat lady said.

"Hot Dilly Dog Buns?" the woman next to her laughed. "That's a cute name. Mine is Mint Condition Cookies. They've got flat little chocolate mints tucked inside green dough. Then I press the top of them with a silver dollar I boil to make clean."

Outside the door, making nervous talk to the guard, was Willie Ruth's mother. She kept straightening her skirt, smoothing her hair, and peeking into the ballroom. I didn't see Willie Ruth anywhere.

When a tall woman in a striped jacket asked everybody to please take their seats, Willie Ruth still wasn't there. I felt funny. I mean, everybody else looked somewhere between a mother and a grandmother. Except one old lady who must have been ninety. Maybe she felt out of place, too. I sat in the back row and looked down at my sneakers.

"Welcome," the lady in the striped jacket said into the microphone. She told us her name was Audrey. "I'm a home economist with the American Baking Congress, sponsors of this Tenth Annual ABC Bake-athon. The ABC represents the companies that make many of the products you will use tomorrow morning when you prepare your prize-winning recipes in this very ballroom." While she listed all the companies, you could hear people suck in their breath, thinking about their recipes and the prize money. I wasn't the only one who wanted it. And you could see them looking over the rest of the group, sizing them up, and wishing everybody else would get appendicitis or desperately homesick or something. Nobody wasted much time looking at me.

Orientation was being told what we were supposed to do the next day. Audrey kept introducing people who explained how the stove worked and the mixer mixed, and how Mrs. This and Mr. That, who we'd recognize because they'd be wearing striped jackets like hers, would help by opening our cans and washing our dishes because we wouldn't have sinks out there on the floor of the Crystal Ballroom.

Everybody was craning forward and I could hardly see from the last row. For a while I tried sitting on my feet, but they went to sleep. Then I could hardly listen for trying to get the pins out.

"The judging area," Audrey was saying, "will be right behind that door," and she pointed to the far end of the ballroom. "And right next to it," where there was a room made of gold curtains, "is the photography area where you will have your picture taken with your creation." Me and my gingerbread smiling for the camera. "We'll take the photograph ahead of time before sending your finished product in to be judged. You'll need to make your recipe twice, once for the judges and once for display. Choose your best one to go in to the judges. That's what they taste and admire. The one on display is just so the rest of us can see what you've done.

"At your cooking stations we've included enough ingredients for three bakings, in case," and she grinned, "you should forget it's in the oven, let it burn once, and need to try again." Sunshine forced its way into the front of my brain and I thought about it burning and Mom looking at the melted sign and crying, and how much she wanted this thirty thousand dollars so we could try again.

"But so that doesn't happen, here's the timer on your range." Audrey gave it a little twist to demonstrate that it wasn't just for show. "And I guess that's all. Except . . ." and she unfurled a big white chef's apron with birthday cakes on it and "Tenth ABC Bake-athon" printed right across the top. "These are for to-morrow. I'll pass them out to you now. Don't forget them in the morning because we'll go straight from breakfast to baking. Wear bright, solid colors if you brought them, for good photographing. And try not to let all the media people bother you. They're here from magazines, newspapers, television stations all over the country to find out about the one hundred best cooks in America."

I felt sick. One hundred best cooks in America? Me? There must be some mistake. The kids in my class had said yuck. I fingered Mom's recipe in my pocket.

"Oh, and one more thing. When you take your finished product in for judging, you must include a signed statement that should be no problem for you. It says, 'I, the undersigned, represent that this food was prepared by me alone from the recipe I submitted to the Tenth ABC Bakeathon.'"

Bur-g, bur-g, bur-g, bur-g, the timer Audrey had twirled went off. *Bur-g, bur-g, bur-g,* it jabbed at us just as the door to the Crystal Ballroom swung open. The sound had startled everybody, but the sight in the doorway was something else. Willie Ruth Jennings was standing there in her silver swimsuit only partly covered up by a fuzzy yellow robe, her birthday cake badge pinned sideways on it. On her head was my Cubs cap. Next to Willie Ruth stood Mrs. Jennings, holding her finger to her mouth saying "Shhhhh," like that would keep people from seeing them. On the other side was my mother, her eyes searching me out, clutching a five-pound bag of sugar under her arm.

I slumped down in my seat and closed my eyes, but then I realized that pretty soon my mom was going to find me and that would just make the agony worse.

As I straightened up I could hear, over the microphone, Willie Ruth talking. She and her mother had walked over to Audrey and the other people in striped jackets.

"Oh, I just can't *tell* you how sorry I am," she was saying, her voice reaching every corner of the ballroom, "but that Florida sun is just hyp*not*ic. I mean, I was having such a good time with these boys I met and the time passed just like *that*."

"Willie Ruth's always been such a fright when it comes to time," her mother said, and somebody turned off the mike.

My mother was still outside the door, looking bewildered. People were filing out past her, talking about tomorrow.

"Did you have a good sleep?" I asked her as I walked up. "Where'd you get the sugar?"

"It wasn't easy," she said, lowering her voice like she was a spy. "This isn't exactly grocery-store row. I had to take a cab to a shopping center."

We sat down in chairs just across from the ballroom door, my knees weak. "Listen, Mom," I started, "about that sugar. It's not possible—your idea about the recipe. I have to sign a thing saying I cooked with the recipe I sent in."

She frowned.

"Besides, Mom, listen, I'm *proud* of its being natural

food. That's what it's all about. No kidding. It's the right thing to do." It was funny, I'd never felt like that before. I'd argued with my mother and all, you know, about wanting to go someplace she didn't want me to go and stuff like that. But now I was telling her what to *do* and what was *right*, like she was the kid, not me.

"I just thought," she tried to explain, "that the fire had changed things. . . . We need—"

"What *about* the fire?" I asked her. It was weird how I felt older than her all of a sudden.

She shook her head and looked up at the people coming out of the ballroom in bunches, laughing and excited. Their laughing seemed to make her even sadder.

"The fire," she said slowly, like talking was hard for her, "I think it may have been for the best. Nothing seemed to be going well at Sunshine. Maybe it was Mr. Corso's hot dogs smelling up the place. Maybe it was the supermarket. Or . . . I don't know. I'd been trying to think of a way out. A lot of stores are closing. Since you were a baby we'd been doing it, and that was too . . ."

Then, all of a sudden, *zap!* My Cubs cap came whipping through the air into my lap.

"You forgot it at the pool," Willie Ruth called, strolling over, "and it looked like you weren't coming back so I used it to shade my nose. Hope you don't mind." She smiled her excellent smile. "I bet that's your mamma," she said, adding a little wicked curve to her mouth.

"Mom," I said, "this is Willie Ruth Jennings. She's making something called Toad in the Hole."

"How'd you know that? I didn't tell you that. Oh, you cute boy, you checked up on me, didn't you?" Willie Ruth said, and my face turned hot. "What are *you* making?" she asked Mom.

"I'm . . . *I'm* not baking anything," Mom said. "It's Mitch. He's making gingerbread—good healthy gingerbread."

Willie Ruth laughed. She laughed like somebody had her down and was tickling her ribs. "Why didn't you tell me? Here I thought you were just a tag-a-long," she howled. "I never dreamed you were *cooking*! And I bet you're here with your mamma's recipe just like me. I never—"

Her mother came rushing out of the ballroom, waving Willie Ruth's apron like a flag. She started fluttering over her daughter, waving the air to clear it of words.

"Willie Ruth, I don't know what comes over you, saying things like that. I've been in there trying to apologize for your behavior. I was worried sick about you. Just worried sick. In this strange place and all . . ."

"Oh, Mamma, don't fuss," Willie Ruth said. *She* clearly was used to telling her mother what to do. And it looked like her mother was used to her doing it. Then she turned back to me. "I'm going out tonight with these guys I met at the pool. Banquet food is like airline food. I just hate it, don't you? I'll see you to-morrow morning . . . Gingerbread Man." And she bounced off laughing, her mother tagging behind.

Mom and I looked at each other and both of us laughed. Boy, was I glad for Willie Ruth Jennings.

"What's your horoscope for today?" I asked Mom.

"I didn't see it," she said, brightening a little more. "What's yours?"

I dug it out of my shoe. " 'Improve relations with friends by having serious talks about important sub-jects.' Mom . . ." She looked me in the eye. "I mean, you've been acting kind of funny and saying things that . . . I mean, you didn't . . . set the fire . . . did you?"

She put her hand to her throat and gasped. "Good grief, no." She started turning the bag of sugar around in her lap, smoothing the edges where it was wrinkled. "I guess it could have seemed that way. The police . . ." Then she put the sugar bag in a big ashtray that was held in the mouth of a gold plaster fish standing on its tail. It wobbled under the weight.

"I'm sorry you were worried," she went on. "Look, Mitch, things were so bad in the store, I did sometimes wish it would just disappear in smoke. But I didn't set it. Honestly. And while I've been . . . worried some

123

about it . . ." She looked away. ". . . I don't really think your father set it, either."

She stood up and walked fast across the lobby, pushing her way through the crowd. Upstairs she got into bed again and pretended, at least, to be asleep.

That night I went to the banquet alone, sitting quietly between the talkative Kiwi Cartwheel Tart from Gary, Indiana, and the very jolly Spinach-Ricotta Pillows from Amarillo, Texas.

10
Smile

BR-R-RING, BR-R-RING, BR-R-RING. THE PHONE BY THE bed woke me. I opened my eyes only wide enough to grab the receiver and stop the noise.

"Good morning," a cheerful voice chirped. "This is your wake-up call. It's seven o'clock. This is a recording." I hung up and pulled the covers over my head.

"Today's no day for ostriches," Mom said brightly and pulled the covers off my face. Then she opened the drapes and the sun came pouring in, practically lapping my face with light.

Mom was already dressed, whipping around like a small tornado—and *smiling*. "It's B-Day," she said. "How's it feel knowing you're going to be spending the morning over a hot stove?"

I blinked. She'd been so up-and-down for the past few days I hardly knew what she might say next.

"Sorry I was asleep when you came in last night. I *meant* to stay awake." She sat down with a pad of paper and started sketching a sailboat in the ocean.

"I talked to your father while you were partying," she went on cheerfully. "He told me the meeting with the fire chief was uneventful, and that he expected a report tomorrow or the next day."

"I bet he said not to worry."

"Right."

"I bet you finally asked him if he set the fire."

"Wrong. Besides, I know he didn't. Anyway, you can't ask somebody you love if they did something like that."

"I did," I told her, feeling awful that I had.

"Well, I don't believe he would do such a thing. Even when the place was on the skids he liked running it. No, it was just bad food and lack of sleep that made me think he might have. Now you get dressed, brush your teeth with the baking soda I brought, and comb the tangles out of those red curls."

She sounded like my mother again. But still, things were different. I had told her the day before what was right and what was wrong, and she had listened.

The band was playing "Keep Your Sunny Side Up, Up," loud and fast at seven forty-five when we walked into the banquet hall for breakfast. Willie Ruth, already eating, was dressed in red and laughing like she was having a wonderful time. I decided it was safer all the way around for us to sit next to the Spinach-Ricotta Pillows woman, who had a kid twelve years old at home in Texas.

We got to choose breakfast from a huge buffet table that even had granola, yogurt, and lots of fresh strawberries for Mom, which surprised her a lot. While we ate, the president of the American Baking Congress gave us a big pep talk about how fabulous we all were and about how great America's food wholesalers and retailers were, too. He told us all to do our very best and then he read something from the Bible that said, "The race is not to the swift, nor the battle to the strong, but time and chance happeneth to them all." And I worried about that. If the race is not to the swift, then who *is* it to? Is everything just luck—broken teeth, fires, and all? Didn't it matter how fast you ran or how hard you tried?

"Mom," I whispered, "would you get a newspaper so I can read my horoscope? I want to know if everything is going to be all right." What I wanted was a good, clear-cut horoscope that said, "Do your best and you will win." Then I'd do my best and I would win. Just like that.

The band had stopped during the speech, but it started back suddenly with a fanfare, a call to arms. All the contestants at my table grabbed their aprons and rushed to get in line for what the speaker called "The Grand March." I grabbed my apron, too, gave Mom a hug, and ran after them, putting it on as I went. If he'd seen me, Coach Kenepker would have kicked me off the hockey team and Lenny would have died laughing. Me in an apron with birthday cakes on it. But I didn't care. Nobody here was laughing. Everybody was scrambling, the music was going like crazy, and what with being scared and excited at the same time, tears filled my eyes, but it wasn't crying.

All the contestants could bring one person to Florida with them free so there were a hundred friends and husbands and kids and at least two mothers lined up on either side of a roped-off aisle. Up ahead I could see lights mounted on a tall stand facing us, and guys up on a platform behind a big TV camera. On the sides, too, relatives were taking pictures with flash cameras. As I looked from side to side for Mom, I got so many flash spots in my eyes I was afraid I'd never see anything but polka dots again.

We filed in, aprons on, two by two, as the band played "When the Saints Go Marching In." Once we were all inside the huge gold-wallpapered Crystal Ballroom, the music stopped and a voice boomed over the loudspeaker, "Ladies and gentleman, to your ranges." The gentleman was me.

The race may not be to the swift, but I ran to find my range, anyway. It was number 38. The band played "Sweet Georgia Brown," and I felt like I should be dribbling a basketball all the way. As I ran, a woman passed me dressed in a native costume of some kind with a long printed skirt and a puffy white blouse.

I wondered if it was her good luck charm and if she was counting on it to make her win.

Number 38 was two ranges from the velvet rope where families were huddled, watching. Everything was laid out for me on the counter—molasses, whole-wheat flour, raisins, walnuts, the carrots to grate. Almost like home.

I opened up the flour, dipped in a measuring cup, and started to hum to myself "Sweet Georgia Brown."

"Hey, Gingerbread Man, I bet you never even tasted Toad in the Hole before." I looked up. Willie Ruth was standing at the range smack in front of mine, beaming. We were going to spend the morning face to face.

"Nope," I told her. "Never have. You know how to make it?"

"Not really," she shrugged. "All that picture taking was nice and all, but you won't believe how I hate to cook. I'm a math person basically," she whispered. "My mamma mailed the whole thing in, recipe, entry blank, and all." She put her hands on her hips and peered down at the recipe like it was written in Chinese.

"Are there any live toads in it?" I asked her.

"Not even dead ones. Just those little shriveled-up precooked sausages in a kind of puffy baked pancake. Mamma says it's an old English recipe, but you couldn't prove it by me." She sighed. "I'm glad, at least, somebody else is doing the dishes."

Just then, a woman with "Family Day Food Editor" on her badge started asking Willie Ruth questions and I watched as she smiled and rattled off the whole my-mamma-taught-me-to-cook-when-I-was-practically-an-*inf*ant speech. Since I'd heard it before, I switched off and started to measure spices into the flour. It was nice and familiar and it felt good to be doing something I really knew how to do.

It wasn't long, though, before people with little pads started coming up to me, too, asking me questions about how come it was I learned to cook, and did I think boys should study more home economics, and did the kids at home tease me about being a cook, and did I ever use cake mixes. I was giving them answers, too. I was telling them everything Mom and Dad had taught me about why whole foods were best and thinking about how they would really be proud of my answers, when I realized I hadn't seen Mom since I came in. I ran my eyes along the crowd, but unless she was hidden by some big guy, she wasn't there at all.

"Well, I started cooking when I was a bitsy baby," I heard Willie Ruth tell some guy from the *Miami Herald*, sounding tired of the whole thing.

"She makes all the good old Southern dishes—pecan

puppies, hush pie . . ." I told the guy who was taking notes from her.

Willie Ruth turned around. "And *he* thinks sugar and dyes and additives will kill you if you don't watch out," she told the food editor wearing a "Kiss the Cook" T-shirt who'd just walked up to me. But just as Willie Ruth started to giggle, I smelled something strange, and smoke, dark and greasy, began to rise from her stove. She grabbed the pan from the heat and dropped it on the counter. I leaned over to see. The precooked sausages were charred hard on the bottom and the smell of the burning filled the air. The reporters moved on.

"I wish I was at home and that I had gone to Marlene Hahn's Sweet Sixteen party," she said. The band played "Dixie."

"Have a good time last night?" I asked.

"Fabulous," she said, still sounding mad. "This hotel has a darling place to dance. Except Mamma was so het up about my being out, she kept poking her head in to check up on me."

By the time I got my first gingerbread out of the oven, Willie Ruth was just getting ready to put her Toad in the Hole in. "I've a mind to ask Mamma to come in and finish this off, since she thought it was such a bright idea," Willie Ruth grumbled. But then when somebody came up to ask a question and take her picture, she smiled and said with an accent heavier than usual, "I'm jus' not used to this ol' electric stove. The one we've got down home is gas. The one my mamma cooked on when she was little was a wood stove and I don't 'spect I could handle that one either." She gave a helper the pan to scrub clean.

The smell around me was of onions and chocolate, molasses, lemon, chicken, and—still, faintly—burned sausage. A man in jeans kneeled on the floor, pointed his camera up, and flashed my picture. "Start stirring something and smile," he said, taking another. Suddenly I felt tired, and realized that the music had stopped.

"*Hsssssssst!* Mitch! *Hsssssssst!*" My mother was standing on a chair behind the velvet rope, waving a newspaper at me. "Mitch, I've got it. You sure you want to know what it says?" she called.

I walked over to her as casually as I could, feeling people stare. "Please don't stand on the chair," I asked her, taking the newspaper and feeling annoyed.

"It's the only way a short person like me can see the whole group," she said, hopping down. "Oh, Mitch, sometimes I think you'd rather have a more conventional mother."

"Oh, no," I told her, wondering if Willie Ruth's mother was what you'd call conventional. "You're OK with me." I started flipping for the horoscope.

"I don't know what you'll think, but it didn't raise my hopes," Mom said. "My horoscope told me to follow my own inclinations and to start a new project that will further my interests, and I've been working on that for a time."

Finally I found it. At home the horoscope is usually in the business section, but this paper had it back with the death notices. That didn't seem like a good sign. "OK, here I am," I said. " 'Gemini (May 21–June 20). This is an ideal day . . .' " I glanced up at her and smiled, " '. . . for recreation with your friends!' Recreation with your friends! What's that supposed to mean? I can't believe it. Am I supposed to go out and jump in the waves? What's the last part? 'Show the world your smile!' I've *been* showing the world my smile all day long, but that's not going to make me thirty thousand dollars richer and save my family from welfare." I felt awful. My horoscope had let me down. "You sure that's when I was born?"

"Listen, we're not all that desperate," Mom said. "Besides, there's still *my* horoscope. I'll work on new projects and see what I can come up with."

Before I had time to ask her what *that* meant, Willie Ruth came tearing up, her bottom lip shaking.

"Oh, Mitch," she said, her eyes welling up, "it's just awful. Worse than awful. It's a disaster, that's what it is." Following close behind her, a striped-jacketed woman was carrying a plate filled with what could only be called a disaster. "What am I going to *do*?" Willie Ruth moaned.

"Don't worry about it," the woman told her. "You're supplied with enough ingredients to make your recipe three times. Just throw this one out and start again."

"I can't," Willie Ruth said. "I burned the sausages for the first batch and had to toss them into the garbage, so I've only got enough left for one more time. They said I have to turn in two, one for judging and one for display." She glared at the striped-jacketed woman like the whole mess had been *her* fault.

We all looked down at the Toad in the Hole, which, instead of being a puffy pancake with sausages in it, looked like a lumpy piece of damp dough somebody had been playing catch with—and missed.

"Well, then," the lady said, wincing only a little, "we'll just patch this one up on the plate as your display dish for all the folks out here to see, and you can bake a fresh one for the judges to make their decision from."

Willie Ruth poked at the stuff on the plate until, at least, none of it was hanging off the edge.

"What happened?" Mom asked her. "Did you drop it?"

"Or throw it?" I asked, which seemed more likely.

"No, it wasn't like that at all," she told us. "It didn't

look so bad when it came out of the oven. Not burned or anything. It may not even have been quite done, but it wasn't awful. So I took it over to the picture place. And the man said wasn't I a pretty little thing and why don't I hold it up right by my face so we can get a good close-up. And, well, I had spent a lot of time drawing on good eyes this morning so I held it up close to my face. And he said a little higher, sweetheart, and I guess I held it up a little too high because it slid right off the plate and into my lap. But it was so hot I stood up and it flopped right off onto the floor and people had been walking on that."

"Did the photographer say he was sorry?" Mom asked her.

"I could have just died," Willie Ruth said. She rubbed her eyes with her fists and the black and blue stuff that was on them smeared so she looked like somebody had really belted her one—or two.

The striped-jacketed lady wandered away with the sad, flat Toad and we watched silently as she set it out on the display counter with the other dishes that were finished. When Willie Ruth's mother, who had been browsing through the display looking at all the baked things and telling people about the days of her Plum Perfection Jam Cake, looked up and saw the thing that was sitting there next to Willie Ruth's name, she yelped so loud that everybody within fifty feet of her looked to see if she'd been stabbed or attacked by a cross hot bun.

She stared frantically at Willie Ruth's stove space, saw it was empty, and then spotted us huddled by the velvet rope.

"Willie *Ruth*, what have they done to our beautiful dish?" she cried, sailing across the ballroom toward us. Mom, seeing her coming, escaped out the door.

"Oh, Willie Ruth," her mother moaned, "how *could* you have . . ." and then she saw her daughter's streaked eyes. "You look a sight. What's wrong with you?"

Willie Ruth straightened up. "Not a thing," she said, like nothing really was. "The first one was just a flop, that's all." She grabbed my arm and pulled me back toward the stoves. "Will you help me make this one, Mitch?" she asked.

"I can't. They make you sign something saying you made it yourself," I told her. "That's one of those things they told us at the meeting you missed. Besides, I've got to make another gingerbread."

"Darn it," she said. "This is just not my day."

"Wait a second. I'll tell you what your horoscope says about today." I pulled out the newspaper. "Let's see, you're a Leo . . ."

"You remembered. You *are* cute. But, you know, that stuff's as silly as Santa Claus and the Easter Bunny together."

"OK, then," I shrugged and started to fold it back up.

"No, go ahead. It can't say any worse than what's happened already."

I read it through to myself and laughed. "Here you go, Willie Ruth. Try this one on for size. 'Study your chores and make plans for improvement. Listen to what relatives say. Avoid risks.' "

"It really says *that*?" she asked, peering over my shoulder. "That's no horoscope. That's my mamma talking." And she stalked off to her stove, ready to open another package of precooked baby link sausages.

Since my horoscope didn't give me any advice to follow, I just took my gingerbread over to be judged as soon as it was cool enough to carry. It looked pretty plain—no pink borders or sprinkles or fancy icing. The guy in the gold-curtained room who took the picture said it looked "substantial," but he didn't tell me to hold it higher. I guess he'd learned his lesson. After the picture taking, my striped-jacketed helper carried the gingerbread off to the judges. I waved goodbye to it and smiled like the horoscope said, but I don't expect the world noticed.

I'd hate to be a food judge, to taste stuff all day and decide which is best. The lady at stove 37 said you had to get your entry in good and early so the judges would still have an appetite. The lady at stove 39 said oh no, get it in last and they'd remember it best when it came time to decide. Mine must have gone in somewhere in the middle and that was that.

I was just getting started on my batch for the display counter when I looked over and saw Mom again.

"I couldn't just sit still and not help," she called. She was waving a poster she'd made on a big sheet of paper. No telling where she'd gotten it.

"This is a 'new project that will further my interests,'" she told me in a loud whisper. "And your interests are my interests."

In fancy black letters edged in red, she'd printed,

WAY, WAY OUT AHEAD

IS MITCH'S

HEALTH NUTTY

GINGERBREAD.

No kidding, I thought, who'd want a conventional mother, anyway. "Show the world your smile," my horoscope had told me. And I did.

11
And the Winner Is...

MY NOSE WAS SUNBURNED. I'D SPENT THE WHOLE AFTER-
noon on the beach collecting shells with Willie Ruth.
The morning had been so long, baking and all, and
the afternoon so hot and lazy that it felt like two days
since I'd slept. I leaned back on the pillows of my
bed to watch TV. Mom had turned it on in the middle
of the six o'clock news and then gone out on the balcony to sketch the shore line. She'd bought a new
book, *Sketching From Nature*.

There was an on-site report of an eight-car collision
on the highway and a helicopter view of traffic tied
up for miles. Then the anchorman said, "Coming up
next. There's a big Bakeathon in our town." And on
the screen over his frozen grin was printed, "Ahead:
Cooking for Cash."

"Hey, Mom," I called. "You know all those pictures
they took this morning? Some of them are going to be
on TV."

"Have you seen my green pencil?" she asked.

After commercials for a discount grocery store and a Miami Chevrolet dealer, the weatherman said it was sunny skies ahead for Florida, and then rolled the temperatures of about a hundred cities, including Chicago where it was twenty-six degrees and snowing.

"Hey, Mom," I called again, when the TV showed the Crystal Ballroom covered with stoves. "Here's a picture some guy took from that tall platform. You can almost tell which one is me." She leaned in the room to look.

The announcer was saying, "One hundred lucky cooks gathered today in the ballroom of the Royal Imperial Towers hotel right here in Miami Beach to compete for fifty thousand dollars in prize money." And there were close-up pictures of people stirring batter, and opening ovens, and holding up their pies to the camera.

"One boy is entered in the contest," the announcer went on. And there I was on the screen, scraping the bowl with my finger and licking the dough like the cameraman had told me to earlier in the day. "Mom!" I yelped, and she hurried into the room. "Twelve-year-old red-head Mitch McDandel of Evanston, Illinois, samples his gingerbread dough that he thinks is finger-licking good. What's more, he brought along his own cheerleader."

They'd taken this picture of Mom holding up her sign with both hands, and you could read every word,

"Way, way out ahead is Mitch's Health Nutty Ginger-bread." Then they showed a lot of people huddled around the display of just-baked foods. "While Mitch's mother may be convinced he's way *way* out ahead, Mitch and ninety-nine other cooks will just have to wait until tonight's award banquet to learn who will bring home the Bakeathon bacon." The anchorman shook his head and chuckled like he thought that was some joke. "And now for sports. Will there be some action on the courts tonight, Johnny?"

"Oh, Mitch," Mom beamed, turning the TV off. "My poster showed up so well. I just bet you win."

The phone rang. "They're calling to tell you ahead of time that you've won. You answer it."

"Hello. This is Mitch McDandel."

"And this is Mitch McDandel's father. How you doing?" he asked. "What's the verdict?"

"Not guilty," I said. "It's Dad," I told Mom. "Did you see me on TV? I was on the six o'clock news."

"No," he said uncertainly. "Not the six o'clock news I saw."

"He wouldn't have seen it. It was just local," Mom said.

"Mom said it was just local news, but we both were in it, me licking a spoon and Mom holding up a poster she'd made."

"No kidding. I just called to wish you good luck."

"Thanks, but I think everything's all judged. There

were a lot of good breads and things. I don't know. Any news about the fire?"

"No, not really. I talked to the fire chief and he said they weren't sure just yet, but they had a clue or two."

"Clue? That makes it sound like a crime."

"Lenny and Aaron have both called to see how you're doing."

"What kind of clue?"

"I don't know. Was it a good day, though, cooking in front of all those people?"

"Sure. It was OK. Tell me more about the fire," I said, but I didn't ask him if he'd set it.

"I'm really not sure, Mitch. All I know is that the police sent some samples of burned floor tile to be analyzed by a lab in Skokie."

"Arson?" I asked him.

"You just forget about the fire, relax in the sun, and I'll pick you and your mom up at the bus at three-thirty tomorrow as planned. I'll keep my fingers crossed for you."

"You want to talk to Mom?"

"No, nothing new since last night. I'll stick to my three-minute limit. See you. Good luck."

"See you. Good luck to you," I told him, but he had already hung up.

In the Bakeathon packet there'd been a check for a hundred dollars for out-of-pocket expenses. Mom had cashed it a week or so before we left home and there was only about twenty-five of it left, but she'd gone out and bought me a tie because I hadn't brought one. "It'll make a much better picture," she said.

So when we went down for the big banquet at seven o'clock, my hair was sitting down as close to my head as I could get it, and I was wearing a red-and-blue-striped neck-choker. But all that didn't matter, I was starved, and I couldn't wait to hear what Dad had called The Verdict.

The banquet was in the Celebrity Room, almost as big as the Crystal Ballroom, and bigger than the banquet room of the night before. The chandeliers in it were huge clusters of pink-and-green metal flowers, with lights that looked like pink candles. There were sixteen chandeliers. I counted, as we waited for all the people to arrive. There was a stage in the Celebrity Room, and the same old band was on it playing nice easy elevator music you didn't have to listen to. The people with striped jackets were still wearing them, and one of the group guided me away from Mom and over to table number nine, which had my name card on it. Mom, he said, had to find a place with the food editors and home economists and other guests. I hoped she'd be all right there, but the minute I thought it, I began to laugh. Me worrying about Mom taking care of herself. I did hope she wouldn't make a fuss, though, when a gooey dessert arrived.

I was just pulling my chair out and eyeing the breadsticks when I heard Willie Ruth call "Gingerbread Man!" from table number ten. And before I could sit down, presto, she was waving her name card at me and whispering in my ear. "I'm moving here," she said, setting her card down at the place next to mine. Palming the card that was already there, she whisked it away and propped it up in front of the place she'd been assigned. "I was surrounded by old ladies who wanted to talk about cooking, and I just couldn't stand it," she said when she got back.

The striped jackets were scurrying about, and the ladies at both tables were talking, heads together, about food and money and children, so nobody noticed that Miranda Howard of Torrance, California, had mysteriously been moved from table nine to table ten, and that Willie Ruth Jennings was sitting in her place.

Suddenly, Willie Ruth grabbed my arm. "Do you know who *that* is?" she said, pointing to the stage. And of course I did. You'd have to live in a desert without an electric socket not to know Gary Conrad and his TV talk show. And what with his stick-out ears and crooked grin, nobody else even looks like him. He was standing behind the band in a huddle with the man who'd given the big speech that morning. They looked out over the audience and then disappeared behind a curtain.

Willie Ruth and I talked about Gary Conrad all through dinner, wondering why he was there and whether we could meet him. She dared me to go backstage and ask for his autograph for her, but I didn't.

"Why, every night I watch him," Willie Ruth said. "Every night, unless I'm doing something else." We talked about the times he'd really made people look silly on his show. He sure did know how to make people squirm. "I love to watch him, but I wouldn't be *on* that program for every last penny in the world," she said.

The Meat Roll Loaf lady from Arkansas City, Kansas, who was sitting next to me, asked if I was feeling sick because I wasn't eating my chocolate cheesecake, and I said no and gave her mine.

People were just tilting back in their chairs after dessert when the speeches started, mostly men and women from the ABC companies thanking other people and telling the cooks how great they all were and how we truly all were winners. Willie Ruth and I were talking instead of listening when the band started up with a furious drumroll fanfare. The lights dimmed, a spotlight turned on the stage, and the fanfare turned into the theme song for Gary Conrad's TV show. He bounded on stage and everybody cheered while he threw open his arms like he was going to hug the whole room.

Then he started singing this song with words somebody had made up to sort of fit the evening, "The most beautiful cooks in the world . . ." The spotlight followed him as he hopped off the stage holding a cordless microphone and waltzed around to every table from one to ten, making gooey eyes at the women. I could have crawled under my chair, it was so embarrassing. When he got to table nine he stopped at Willie Ruth and kissed her hand. She didn't giggle. She just looked paralyzed. He saw me slumped down in my chair, and said into the mike—stopping the song in mid-note—"And what have we here? Are you one of the one hundred cooks, young man?"

"Yes, sir," I said so soft the microphone didn't even pick it up.

"And hardly able to get a word in edgewise, I see," he went on. "Are you the only boy cooking?" He poked the microphone at my mouth.

"Yes, I am," I said, "and the only man, too." What I meant was that there weren't any men in the Bake-athon that year, but whatever I said sounded funny and everybody laughed.

"How's it feel to be the only . . . man . . . among a hundred women?"

I could feel the hair on the back of my neck creep, I was so scared. The microphone was practically brushing my teeth. I took a deep breath. "Lonely," I said. And he roared.

"You're not one in a hundred, kid, you're one in a million." And everybody clapped.

After he finished the song he stopped at the judges' table and made them all stand up. When he asked one of them what the judging had been like, she said, "We had a terrible time," and he cut her off by saying, "Food that bad, huh?" "Oh, no," she said, embarrassed, "it was all so *good* we had a terrible time deciding."

"A likely story," he said, moving back on the stage. "And that, ladies and gentlemen, is why the judges had Alka Seltzer with their meals instead of water."

People laughed. But I think they would have laughed at anything, they were so nervous. He drew some envelopes out of his pocket and said, "If you think I'm going to hurry through this you're wrong." And he didn't. He was slow as molasses on a cold day.

First, he gave out the one-thousand-dollar checks. One of them went to a veterinarian from Boston who "cooked quick" in a microwave oven she kept at her office. The last of the thousand-dollar checks went to the ninety-year-old woman I'd seen the first day. Gary Conrad had a hard time with her because she was too old to make fun of and she didn't want to stop talking. Everybody liked her, though, because she told the names of all her great-great grandchildren.

"And now," he said, with more drumroll going, "we

move from the big bucks to the bigger bucks. The five-thousand-dollar prizes go to best-of-class contestants." When he'd handed out the best-dessert prize and the best-bread prize, I was feeling discouraged because I hadn't won anything and what if I didn't get the thirty thousand dollars and had to go home with nothing?

"And the final five-thousand-dollar, best-of-class award for the best main dish goes to"—and the drums went *brrrrrruuuuuummmm*—"a most unusual recipe" —*brrrrrruuuuuuuuum*—"with a most unusual name"— *brrrrrruuuuuum*—"baked by a most unusual lady . . . Willie Ruth Jennings from Murfreesboro, Tennessee!"

"That's my *baby*," Willie Ruth's mother shrieked from the back of the room.

The spotlight riveted on table number ten and everybody there blinked into it, but nobody stood up.

"Oh," Willie Ruth barely peeped in the dark, "do you believe this?"

"Over here!" I shouted and the spotlight swept across the tables looking for Willie Ruth. "Stand *up*," I told her, and she got to her feet just as the frantic beam of light reached her. "Go up on the stage!" I said, giving her a little push.

She looked so pretty on the stage that people were going ah and oh and stuff. She kept saying, "Oh, I'm just so excited. My mamma must be so tickled. I'm just so excited."

"You think it's exciting for you. It's exciting for me just to give it to you," Gary Conrad said. I thought she might say, "But actually, I'm a math person," but she didn't.

"You're mighty young," he said. "How long have you been cooking?"

"Oh," she said, "my mamma taught me to bake when I was practically a baby . . ." And I was the only one in the audience who laughed. She told him about Toad in the Hole and how it was a traditional English recipe and all, and I kept wondering what would have happened if the judges had seen the one out there on display with rug fuzz on it instead of the one she finally turned in.

The women around me looked stunned. They clearly didn't think the glop on display deserved a prize. "Besides," one of them whispered, "she isn't *serious* about cooking." And when she got back to the table they glared at her and then smiled glum smiles, waiting and scared, but not really expecting anything. We'd all got this far without getting a prize, why should this one be any different?

"This is the craziest thing that ever happened to me," Willie Ruth said, sinking into her chair. "Gary Conrad gave me a kiss."

The drummer, whose hands must have been plenty tired by then, started drumming and the trumpeter joined in and Gary Conrad waved the big prize check in the air. "If you've got good enough eyes you can see who it's written out to," he said, flashing it back and forth while everybody craned their necks.

"I've got a feeling," the Meat Roll Loaf lady said, "that I'm not going to be Miss America."

"The big prize winner this year is for . . . a bread," Gary Conrad said.

That's me, I thought. That's me! I could hear people all around moaning because they'd made apple pan dowdy or turkey-lurkey casserole and that let them out.

"The big prize winner is . . . somebody who had to come a long way to get here," he said.

I did! I did! I thought, clinging to the edge of the table.

"And the big prize winner is at table number nine!" I could hear my heart pound. The spotlight turned on us, full and bright, making an island of light.

"The prize winner—the name on this check for thirty thousand dollars—is Miranda Howard of Torrance, California!"

There was a shriek at table number ten, and after another wild search, the spotlight landed at last on Miranda Howard, her face in her hands.

I couldn't believe it. I almost couldn't believe it. I hadn't won anything at all. I waited for him to say he'd made a terrible mistake. The Meat Roll Loaf woman wiped tears from her eyes. And Willie Ruth said, "Mitch, I'm just so awfully sorry."

Up on the stage Miranda Howard couldn't explain to Gary Conrad why she had been sitting at the wrong table. He asked her what her recipe was called and she said, "Rye Not? Spelled N-O-T, because I thought that was kind of funny."

"I can't imagine rye," Gary Conrad told her, and she laughed nervously.

"What it is," she said, "is a loaf of dark rye bread made with yogurt. And it's tied in a big knot with sea salt sprinkled on top. It's got a really great texture. I've entered this contest every year since it started ten years ago," she went on. "Once I sent in an apple pie with cheddar cheese in the crust. Once I sent in a banana pie with a chocolate crust and once a chocolate pie with banana in the crust. I kept sending in pies. Then both my children turned health food, so this year I made rye bread. And that was my lucky recipe—good healthy rye bread. Rye Not?" she asked, and there was polite applause. He asked her what she was going to do with all that money and she said pay for her children's college educations.

I hadn't even met Miranda Howard, but she had beat me at my own game. I think I wouldn't have felt so bad if she'd made Chocolate Pudding Cake with butterscotch chips or a Hot Dog Casserole with packaged mashed potatoes. I'd just lost all chances for winning the money for Sunshine and lost them because of another natural food recipe. I felt awful.

When the lights came up, everybody at our table was smiling bravely like their mothers had taught them when they were little, everybody except Willie Ruth, who still wore a puzzled frown like she'd just woken up from a very strange dream. Our mothers came up at the same time. Hers was bubbling. Mine was simmering.

"We surely did it, baby doll," Mrs. Jennings said. "We surely did."

"It was," Mom told me, "a ridiculous decision. I can't believe your recipe wasn't better than that yogurt rye bread. Sounds very dry."

The two mothers didn't speak to each other at all. Suddenly, they stopped talking altogether and stared just over my head at something that seemed to be just too much for words. I turned around and there he was, Gary Conrad, smiling his famous crooked grin. A dazzling Hollywood-type woman stood next to him, beaming.

"Well, congratulations to you all," he said, rubbing his hands together. "I'm taking a big chance, aren't I, coming down here when the money's all been handed out. I must be on a lot of ladies' hit lists." He chuckled.

We all gaped and waited. He turned to me.

"As for you, young man. Tell me about yourself.

What did you enter in this contest that lost so resoundingly?"

Well, I knew that speech as well as Willie Ruth knew her practically-a-baby one. I'd said it all morning. So I gave him the big natural food talk like he was just some ordinary guy.

"A red-headed boy cook who doesn't eat sugar candy," he said. "Beautiful!"

"Excuse me?" Mom said.

"You his mother?"

"I am."

"Excellent," he went on, all business. "I'd like your son . . . uh . . ."

"Mitch," she said.

"Mitch, to be on my show this Tuesday night—that's day after tomorrow. We'll talk about the Bakeathon, and it'll be nice and current. I'd like to have him make something on the show—some health food thing. Tossed soybeans and seaweed, you know. It'll have to be something he can make quick. We'll give him ten minutes, total, interview and cooking. I suppose he can manage that without you? We'll fly you both to L.A. from . . ."

"Chicago?"

"Chicago, marvelous. All expenses taken care of, of course, and a four-hundred-dollar talent fee. Gloria here," he said, nodding to the beautiful woman next to him, "will take care of the details. Nice meeting you, Mrs. . . . uh . . ."

"McDandel."

"McDaniels." He stuck out his hand.

"No, thank you," she told him. "I think we'll skip that honor."

"You're kidding!" Willie Ruth shrieked.

"Mr. Conrad," Mom told him, "you clearly regard Mitch as a kind of freak, which is doubtless how you'd present him to your audience. And I find nothing at all strange about a young boy who eats and cooks well. I'm sorry, but I think you'd make fun of him."

"I'll be on your show," Willie Ruth said, opening her violet eyes very wide. "*I* won a prize."

"No, thanks, sweetheart," he said, turning to her. "As the lady said, I'm looking for somebody"—he shrugged—"different. What's different about a girl who cooks?"

"But I *don't* cook," Willie Ruth told him. "I *hate* to cook."

"Willie *Ruth!*" her mother said, shocked. We were gathering a crowd.

"You could have fooled me," Gary Conrad said. "Even so, there's no news to that either. Lots of pretty girls hate to cook."

Willie Ruth turned to me. "I'll give you my five thousand dollars for your TV show."

Gary Conrad laughed. "Sorry, my pretty child, but

the offer's just not transferable." He turned to Mom. "Is that final?" he asked, and Mom was just about to say it sure was. I know when Mom looks like that she means it.

"No," I told him, "it's not." I put my hand on her arm. "We'll talk it over. Is tomorrow too late to let you know?"

"I'm flying out tonight," he said, grinning at Mom, wondering how she was taking this. "But Gloria's staying through tomorrow. You can talk with her before you leave."

"No kidding, though," I told him, folding my arms to make myself look as important as possible, "I won't come if you're going to treat me like . . . like a talking dog."

"So, you've watched the show?" He looked amused. "Fair enough. I'll treat you as a serious person. It's agreed, then?"

"Not quite," I said, glancing at Mom, who looked like she'd just swallowed a gray cloud. "We'll talk about it and let you know tomorrow morning."

"I'm in room 777," Gloria said, drawing the numbers in the air with her finger. "And I'm checking out at eleven."

They turned and made their way slowly through the crowd, people stopping them every few feet for autographs. "Why didn't you give *me* the money?" a woman crowed.

"Mitch McDandel, how could you talk to Gary Conrad like that? Now he'll never let you on his show," Willie Ruth cried. "I can't *stand* it! I declare, you're nutty as a fruitcake!"

"Mitch McDandel," Mom said, "if you really want to be *on* that program, I quite agree with Willie Ruth. 'Nutty as a fruitcake,'" she said, shaking her head. "I couldn't have put it better myself."

12
Surprise!

THE TAKEOFF FROM MIAMI INTERNATIONAL AIRPORT was easier than the one from Chicago, so easy that Mom wasn't even nervous. Actually, she was too mad to be nervous. The night before we'd had a big argument. The more she'd said no to me, the more I'd been sure that being on the show was the right thing to do, and the more I was positive Dad would agree with me. He'd want the new Sunshine to open with a bang, and what could be louder or more boffo than the Gary Conrad Show? But she wouldn't listen. "No," she said flatly, "I'm not going to discuss it further, and that's that."

I was so certain that once I made her listen, I could convince her it was a *perfect* idea, that before we left the hotel I went to one of those phones in the lobby and called Gloria in room 777. She told me she'd make all the arrangements for two and call me at home that night. Just as we took off I told Mom what I had done.

"So you've said you'll do it." Mom sighed, and

looked at me like I'd brought home straight F's on my report card. "What now? It's tomorrow, you know, that he wants you there, so it'll be 'nice and current.' What do you plan to do, just gather up some old jokes from Lenny, fly off to California tomorrow morning, and have them rolling in the aisles by afternoon? Mitch, you are a good kid, but, unlike Lenny, you are not the show-business type."

A week before, I wouldn't have dreamed of doing something that important when Mom told me not to. But I thought I was right and I was sure I could explain.

The plane tilted and down below you could see the ocean and the tall hotels and the swimming pools filled with salt water. "You know what it'll be like?" Mom went on, looking out at the blue. "It's not going to be glamorous at all." She pointed her hand at me and started mimicking Gary Conrad. " 'Looks normal, doesn't he, folks—like a red-blooded, red-headed, freckle-faced American boy—but, would you believe, he doesn't eat cotton candy or hot dogs or chocolate bars or drink Coca-Cola. And take a look at the funny stuff he cooks, tossed soybeans and seaweed. What a freak.' "

"He promised me he wouldn't," I told her. "Besides, it's true. I don't eat those things. I never have. *Please* listen." I grabbed her arm and got her to look me in the eye for once. "I'm doing it," I explained slowly, "because it'll be a plug."

"A *plug*?" she asked, so loud that the stewardess, giving her talk on how to exit if we crashed, stopped to see if something was the matter.

"You know, a plug," I whispered. "They have them on talk shows all the time. People go on the shows just to plug records they've made or movies they're in or books they've written or acts they're going to perform in Las Vegas or something. They must think it's going to do them some good or they wouldn't be on the show to plug whatever it is they're plugging."

Mom stared at me like we'd never met and she wondered who was sitting next to her. "What is it," she asked, "that you are planning to . . . plug?"

"Sunshine," I told her, amazed that she couldn't guess. "I'll tell them how it burned and that we're going to open it grander than ever, with improvements and all. It would have been better if I'd won some money to do it with, but when we do open again, people who saw it on TV will rush in like those ocean waves." I smiled at her and scratched my head, waiting for her to smile back, suddenly understanding. "*Now*, what do you think?"

Mom looked out the window at the huge puffs of clouds and bit her lip. "Do you know what your horoscope is for today?" she asked me.

"You didn't read it to me this morning," I told her, "and I didn't look. I've decided it's like Willie Ruth said, half Santa Claus, half Easter Bunny. Even if you believe in it, that doesn't mean it will bring you what you want."

"It doesn't *bring*," she said, surprised that I should say it did. "It tells you how you should act on certain days to get what you want. Here's mine." And she got the paper out of her purse to show me. " 'Today is ideal for telling others what changes you have in mind.' That's the important part." She took a deep breath. "As it happens, I do have some changes in mind."

"Does that mean we shouldn't go to California so I can be on the talk show and talk about Sunshine?" It didn't sound like that's what it meant, but then horoscopes are tricky. You can make them mean things they don't say.

"I've been dreading telling you this. But I didn't know you were counting on it that much. Your father agreed with me the other night on the phone. We're not going to open Sunshine again."

The stewardess walking down the aisle stopped and asked me if I felt all right. I must have looked green.

"Not going to open Sunshine?" I asked, when I could breathe again. "Not the way it is, of course, but aren't we going to fix it back up?"

"No, we aren't. I told you I was tired of it before, remember?"

"But Sunshine is like a part of the family. You can't

give it up just because you're tired of it."

She looked the other way.

The plane hit a bump in the air and the "Fasten Your Seat Belt" sign flashed on. "We've run into a little unexpected turbulence here," the captain said over the loudspeaker, "so we're going to delay meal service awhile and ask that you remain seated with your seat belts fastened." We were both quiet for a few minutes, riding the bumps.

"If we don't have Sunshine, what is there?" I asked finally.

"We'll manage. You don't need to worry. Everything will be all right."

"Were you going to give it up even before the fire?"

"I was ready to. It was your father who wanted to keep it. But he did agree to talk to some people I found who thought they might want to take over the place. That was the night before the fire, remember, when he and I went out in that cold night. We showed this vegetarian couple the store and all our not-very-prosperous-looking papers."

"Did they want it?"

"They said they'd think it over." She just sat there awhile looking out the window, which was by then completely covered with a gray curtain of cloud. "The reason I stupidly worried about the fire and your father was that he went back into the shop to look for his keys while the rest of us waited outside. It took him a long time to find them. That seems like a very long while ago. I've decided something else. I've decided that what I *do* want is a job, a nine-to-five job, Monday through Friday, with vacations. I want a job that won't give me ulcers even though I eat good food."

"I bet that's not the kind of job Dad wants. He always said he liked being his own boss."

"No," she said, "it isn't. We're different people. Nor," she said, "is my nonexistent nine-to-five the kind of job you can go on the Gary Conrad Show and 'plug.' I don't know what your father plans to do. The only thing you would have to plug on that show would be yourself. And if you want to do that, I suppose you may, but *I'm* not going with you. I'm just not up to it." She leafed through the newspaper without reading it. Opening the entertainment pages wide, she said, "Look, TV isn't the real world. It won't solve anything."

"I know," I told her, and looked out the window for land, but there wasn't any.

All the way to Chicago the air was bumpy. It wasn't the kind of bumpy that rocks you to sleep, but we both closed our eyes anyway so we wouldn't have to talk.

When the stewardess offered us lunch, Mom shuddered and said no, thank you. I poked at mine. It was beef stew.

If Dad says no, I thought, I won't go to California.

Face it, I thought, if Dad says no, I *can't* go to California. I clenched my eyes tight and wished we were heading back toward Florida instead of away from it. Everything there seemed more real than Evanston did. I didn't want to land.

We circled Chicago in a holding pattern because it was snowing and the planes were backed up. We went around for thirty minutes, but we finally broke through the clouds to land. And after rescuing our bags from the big luggage turntable in the airport, we ran for the bus to Evanston.

The bus wasn't there, so we had to wait. Those were just about the coldest fifteen minutes I've ever waited anywhere. Mom and I were still dressed for Florida, and Chicago wasn't Florida by a long shot. We talked about how cold it was.

Inside the bus, finally, the heaters blasted us, and as we thawed we talked about how good it was to feel warm again.

The man behind us on the bus smoked like a steel mill, and together Mom and I scowled about it.

"Do you know," I asked Mom, "what 'trash' is in Pig Latin?"

She grinned, not mad at me now. "No, my friend," she said, "what *is* 'trash' in Pig Latin?"

"Ash-tray," I said, and we laughed.

Dad was waiting when the bus pulled in at the Barrington Hotel. We both hugged him at the same time.

"I didn't win anything," I told him right off, in case he'd been counting on it.

"When I didn't hear last night," he said, "I assumed you weren't bringing home the crock pot at the end of the rainbow. We better run for the car before you two freeze."

I'd wanted to go in the hotel to see the goldfish, to kind of put off going home. It would have been a dumb thing to ask, though, so I didn't.

"Was it hot in Florida?" he asked Mom. "You look rested."

"Yes," she said, "it was warm."

What about Sunshine? I wanted to ask him. Is it really gone for good? Who set the fire? I need to know. I know you didn't. Instead, I said, "I can hardly wait to see Lenny and Aaron."

"What will you tell them?" Dad asked, as we turned into the driveway.

"I'll tell them about the sunlamp over the john in the hotel and about Willie Ruth Jennings and her Toad in the Hole. I will also tell them about the mountain in the swimming pool with the waterfall."

"That," Dad said, "is one conversation I wouldn't miss for the world."

He didn't miss it, either, and it happened sooner than I thought. The second we opened the front door, Lenny and Aaron flicked on the lights and the radio, and leaped out like they were on springs, yelling,

"Surprise!" as if it was my birthday. They'd come there straight from school and waited to explode when the door opened.

"Where," Lenny asked, "is my thousand bucks?"

"My dad told my mom you sure are some go-getter," Aaron said.

The music played on the radio and it was like everything was fine. I scratched my head and stood there, happy to be home. Dad brought out a big bowl of fruit and some cheese and banana bread. He'd made the peanut-butter-carob balls that I like, too. "I thought we'd do without the famous gingerbread this time," he said.

"If it didn't taste so good, I'd never eat it again," I laughed. Then, as we sat around the dining room table, I told them about the whole trip. I showed them the seashells I'd found that looked like turkey wings and told them about the salty swimming pool and the Rancho Taco Puffs and the Root Beer Pound Cake and the Rye Not? and about how Gary Conrad had MC'd and how Willie Ruth had changed seats at the banquet and the spotlight had gotten lost.

I noticed that Lenny, sitting next to me, was staring at me funny, with a look like I was turning green in front of his eyes or something.

I didn't think he was jealous. It was like he was only half listening to my story. "What's wrong?" I asked him.

"Oh, nothing—nothing—no kidding, nothing. But there's something I've *got* to tell you." I waited for him to go on. "Uh, later," he said, glancing toward Mom.

On the radio, the music stopped, and we could hear Leroi Rupert open a creaky cellar door, and then, as a mumbling, growling monster, clump louder and louder up the cellar steps and breathe over the air, "This is WOGR, ogre, 1440 on Amplitude Modulation. Should you move the dial from that magic number, your scintillating brain will dissolve into instant mashed potatoes." And the heavy cellar door slammed shut. The music began again. We all laughed. Leroi Rupert is OK.

"We met Gary Conrad," I said. "After the banquet."

"Did he sign your gingerbread?" Lenny asked.

"You're not going to believe this." I looked at Mom. She was watching Dad. "But Gary Conrad asked me to be on his television program tomorrow night."

"You're kidding!" Lenny yelped. "You're gonna do it, aren't you? What are you gonna talk about?"

"You putting us on?" Aaron asked, and I shook my head. "Gary Conrad does wild things sometimes. Maybe you should wear your hockey uniform. Then if he embarrasses you or something you could just pull down the mask."

"The only time I saw a kid on that show," Lenny said, "except for an actor-type kid, was this girl who played an aluminum cello underwater. They showed a videotape and talked about how she used nylon string instead of gut because it didn't stretch. I remember she was on with this really great old-time jazz singer and a man who invents electronic games. He gets a lot of variety on that show, Gary Conrad does. You want some good jokes?" Then he frowned and whispered, "I've *got* to talk to you."

"What does he want you to do on the show?" Dad asked.

"I don't know. Make some health food things, I guess," I told him, thinking maybe the hockey mask wasn't a bad idea.

"And you gave your permission?" he asked Mom.

"No," she said, "I didn't."

"Geez," Lenny moaned, "I'd give my right arm to be on that show. Or anyway, my left, since that's the one I write with."

"Mitch, however, told him yes," Mom went on.

Dad raised his eyebrows. No one said anything.

"Mom won't go with me," I told him. "Will you go tomorrow? Please?"

"To California?" he asked, still not used to the whole idea. He glanced over at Lenny and Aaron. "Let's talk about it later. You guys want some more food here?" he asked, handing them a half-empty bowl of orange slices.

"Oh, no thanks," Aaron said. "I've got homework.

Got a diorama book report due and I haven't read the book." He hurried over to get his coat. "Hockey practice is tonight. You coming?"

"Not tonight," I told him. "Are you?"

"Yeah," he said. "I'm going to wear this special protector in my mouth. My mom doesn't like the idea at all," he said, "but . . ." And you could see him realize that he could be talking about my folks. His voice trailed off, ". . . but my dad says I should do it."

Lenny pushed back his chair and followed Aaron. "Let me know what happens and I'll tell everybody at school," he said loud. Under his breath, he mumbled, "Can I tell you something private?"

"Sure," I told him, "I'll call you later." I really wanted to get it all straight about Sunshine and the fire and the trip to California—about it all. I didn't want to talk to Lenny. "Later," I told him. "OK?"

"OK, sure. But don't forget. It's *urgent*."

When the door slammed and there were just the three of us, it was quiet, except for a jeans commercial on the radio. Dad turned it off.

"Please," I said to Dad, "before we talk about the TV show, I've got to know about Sunshine. Tell me why it burned and what's going to happen to it now."

"Tall order," Dad said. He got up and started taking the plates to the kitchen. "I can tell you that an inspector from the state fire marshal's office sent some pieces of the store's burned floor tile and baseboard out to be analyzed by a private lab. But I can't tell you what they found because I don't know. All I know for sure is that there was a fire, that almost everything was destroyed, and that our insurance is up to date.

"And I didn't tell you about Saturday and Sunday, did I?" He laughed. "Mr. Corso had all his relatives in over the weekend to scrub and paint. His nephew dropped the neon hot dog and broke it into a thousand pieces and I thought Corso was going to crack the poor kid on the head with a french frier. He even let me help them clean for a while to keep me busy—three or four hours. There was nothing I could do about Sunshine, since it's all boarded up."

"But Mr. Corso said you and Mom burned Sunshine," I said. "How could you be nice to him?"

"How *could* you, Ralph?" Mom said, astonished. She put down the slice of banana bread she was nibbling.

"I explained to him why we were there the night before the fire," Dad told her. "We were talking to some people who were interested in buying out Sunshine," he said to me.

"I know," I told him.

"Ready to talk about California?" he asked.

I scratched my head and thought. "No, I've got to know what will happen next at Sunshine. Mom says you're not going to open Sunshine again. Is that right?"

"Oh, Mitch," Dad said, sitting back down at the table with us. "It's the same answer as before. I don't know. I've been thinking about it, but I just don't know yet. I think your mother doesn't want to open it again."

"Your mother *doesn't* want to open it again," Mom said.

Dad smiled at her. "Your mother, I think, wants to branch out."

"Your mother *does* want to branch out." She smiled back at him.

The phone rang. "That's probably Lenny and his secret message," I said, running to answer it. But it wasn't.

"Hi!" the voice said brightly. "Is this Mitch?"

"Yes," I said, "this is Mitch McDandel."

"Fabulous. This is Gloria. Remember me, from the Gary Conrad Show?"

How could I forget? "I remember."

"I'm getting things all set up for you and your mother. You want to leave Chicago at eight-thirty tomorrow morning or at ten-ten?"

"Can you hold on a second?" I asked her. "Hey, Dad," I called. "You want to leave for California at eight-thirty tomorrow morning or ten-ten?"

He looked at Mom.

"Oh, go ahead," she said. "It's your turn for a warm vacation. Maybe you'll discover something wonderful for us away from this wretched snow. Maybe any-thing! Meantime, I'll go out job hunting tomorrow."

The doorbell rang. And rang. Nobody was moving so I ran to get it.

"Dad," I called, "you talk to Gloria. Tell her ten-ten, OK?"

It was Lenny at the door. He had a paper bag in his hand.

"Come on in," I told him. "I'm sorry I didn't call. We got to talking."

"That's OK. Listen, I gotta get back home. But I had to see you a minute."

"Something important?" I asked him, scratching my head.

"What I wanted to tell you before . . . I mean, I've gotten to be a kind of expert. . . ."

"You've written down a lot of food jokes for me to tell on the show tomorrow night? Listen, I probably couldn't tell them as good as you do. I told Mom about the Pig Latin ashtray but I think she only laughed because I'm her kid."

"No, it's not jokes. You *are* going tomorrow? That's great. Actually, that's why I'm here. I mean, if you're going tomorrow you've got to have this tonight." He looked down at the bag. "I feel like those TV com-mercials where people tell guys they've got bad breath."

I covered my mouth with my hand.

"No, it isn't that, though."

"Why are you whispering?" I asked him.

"I'm whispering because your mom doesn't like killing things."

"What do you want to *kill*?" I asked him, wondering what the punch line to this joke was going to be.

"Look, it may be my fault. It probably is. But, Mc-Gingerbread, when you were telling us about Florida, I saw you scratching your head and I looked on the edge of your collar, and I hate to tell you this, but you've got lice."

"Lice?" I hissed back. Suddenly my whole head felt like it was alive with whole hockey teams of lice. I could feel them clinging and skidding and spitting. "What am I going to do?" I asked him.

He slipped a bottle out of the bag and handed it to me secretly, though nobody was watching us. "It's lice-killer shampoo. My mom got three bottles of it and this one we never got to." He watched me scratch my head and grinned. "I didn't want to see you on nationwide TV with lice crawling around for the close-ups. Didn't fit the health food image somehow. Though, come to think of it, Gary Conrad would probably have loved it. It would have been a first."

I stuck the shampoo inside my shirt. "Thanks," I whispered.

"It's OK," he said. "Nobody wants to be called a

louse, but they sure do have a way of hanging in there."

"Twelve-fifteen," I heard Dad say, "at the luggage claim, United Airlines. I think this is all astonishing, but we'll see you there, Gloria."

"I hope you didn't give them to anybody else," Lenny said.

"Oh, my gosh," I yelped.

"Mitch, what's wrong?" Mom called out.

"You OK?" Dad asked.

"Sure. Sure. It's OK!" I yelled to them. Then I turned back to Lenny. "You know that Willie Ruth I told you about?" I said, as quiet as I could.

"The girl with the long black hair and violet eyes who talked southern? Yeah."

"Well, when she left Florida this morning for Murfreesboro, Tennessee, you know what she was wearing? She was wearing my blue Cubs cap."

"Oh, my gosh," he said, laughing. "Go wash your hair."

I slammed the door.

"Mitch," Mom called, "what on earth was it?"

"It was just Lenny," I called back, "with another one of his lousy jokes." And, scratching my head, I ran for the shower.

13

And My Guest Is...

SO THAT'S HOW I CAME TO BE SITTING, BUGLESS, IN THE television city greenroom of Studio A, waiting to be on the Gary Conrad Show. On the TV monitor mounted in the wall I could see Walt Milliken, the basketball superstar, walk between the curtains, smiling and waving to cheers. He was like six feet seven. Gary Conrad, who came up to his shoulder, looked like a twerp.

I walked over and turned the sound up. "Do you care?" I asked Alexandra, the zoo person. She shrugged, so I turned it up still louder.

"—sportswriters this weekend voted him the nation's number one basketball player, what do you think of that, no kidding?" Gary Conrad said, tossing the basketball he was holding at Walt Milliken. Milliken caught it with his fingertips and, without looking, flung it over his shoulder toward a net that was set up on the stage. *Swish*, it slipped through and bounced out into the audience. They loved it.

So Conrad said, "Like, how can they say you're best, Milliken, when you fouled out before half-time in that last game with the Celtics and only made seventeen points? No kidding, you think you're the best?"

Milliken slam-dunked the ball. "No such thing as best," he said. "There's always somebody running faster, jumping higher. I do the best I can. Let those guys who gave the award say I *am* the best. I'm not gonna tell you that."

Gary Conrad's face fell. You could tell he wanted this guy to be a peacock, to fight with him. But Milliken was cool. Gary Conrad rolled his eyes, shrugged, and gave his famous this-guy-is-a-nut look straight into the camera. "And now a word or two from the folks who make all this . . ." He twirled his hands around like he couldn't think of a word to describe it. ". . . possible." Taking careful aim with the ball, he tossed and missed the basket by a mile.

My time had to be coming soon. Out there somewhere in the audience Dad was sitting, but that didn't make it any easier. My heart was racing. They had coffee on a little table, and Pepsi, but I didn't drink either one. I was just beginning to think how thirsty I really was when the door burst open again. Gloria was in a hurry this time.

"Milliken isn't working out. Gary cut him short and the commercials are on. Come on, Mitch, let's go. You're on right after the Arrid Extra Dry." She leaned over as we walked to give me some advice. "Stay cool now, and have fun. Remember, just forget the camera. The one that's on, though, is the one with the red light glowing. Don't let Gary make you mad or anything. Tell lots of stories about the contest. Funny stories. Gary loves funny stories."

The Toad in the Hole on the floor? I thought. No, not that. Lice? Double no. Rye Not? Because I don't want to, I thought. Suddenly I realized I didn't have *anything* to say. My throat was dry.

I couldn't hear how Gary Conrad had introduced me, but I did hear the big round of applause from the audience just before Gloria gave me a shove through the bright green curtains.

It was like another world on the other side. The air was so heavy with heat that the people staring and clapping could have been a mirage. The lights were staring, too, and the orchestra was playing "If I Knew You Were Coming I'd Have Baked a Cake." I could make out the cameras Gloria had told me about. The red light shone on the forehead of the one facing me, so I knew it was on and that millions of people had just watched me try to push my hair flat.

Gary Conrad, Walt Milliken, and the actress named Dawn sat on a platform that had two walls painted behind it like windows looking out over Los Angeles. I looked into the audience for Dad.

"Oh, Mitch," Mr. Conrad called, "we're over here,

not out there." He waved me onto the stage. "Climb up and tell us all about it." The chair next to him was empty. I climbed up the two steps and I sat. What was "all about it"? Gloria had given me a lot of advice, but she hadn't said anything about "tell us all about it."

But Gary Conrad forged ahead. "No kidding, one hundred cooks from sea to shining sea were there, cooking up a storm. I handed out fifty thousand smacks in prize money," he said, grinning the crooked grin and rocking back and forth in his chair. "And young Mitch here was the only boy in the Bakeathon, outnumbered ninety-nine to one. What do you think of that?" People clapped at me being outnumbered.

The camera, its little red light on, peered at me. I wished for the hockey mask Aaron had said I should wear to pull over my red face.

"Tell the folks what your recipe is called."

"Health Nutty Gingerbread," I told the red light, since I guessed that's where most of the "folks" were. And then I told the story about making up the recipe and how honey and molasses are more nourishing sweeteners than refined sugar and how carob doesn't have all the caffeine in it that chocolate does, when Gary interrupted me.

"You play basketball, too, kid?" he asked. "Like Walt Milliken?"

"I couldn't begin to play basketball like Walt Milli-ken," I said, sneaking a fast look over at him. I mean, I'd been sitting right *next* to him, and I couldn't even ask him for an autograph.

The audience laughed. I took a deep breath. "I play hockey," I said, surprised I could still speak. "I'm goalie on a team called the Jets." I tried to think of something funny. Lenny would have. "Our last game, my friend Aaron lost a tooth, but they fastened it back in."

"That's the breaks," Gary Conrad said, and started fooling with the pencils on the desk in front of him.

"You gonna win your league?" Walt Milliken asked. I looked at him again. He was smiling.

"I dunno. We're going to try." That's not a funny story, I thought. Very soon they're going to put on Arrid Extra Dry again and I won't have told them what I wanted to.

"Maybe your friend will get a new tooth and it'll be even prettier than the last one," Dawn said. "I got new teeth." The camera moved in closer to show her absolutely perfect smile. She flung her long feathered scarf over her shoulder and one of the pink feathers drifted up and then down to my shoulder. "Aren't they beautiful! They're all capped," she said as the camera blinked its eye at them, "at about the cost of a Mercedes. I've wanted to be an actress since I was *your* age," she cooed, pointing her long-nailed fingers at me. "It was a hard fight, but . . ." She glowed, letting everybody finish the sentence in their minds.

"Not everybody wants to fight their way to the top," I said, remembering the doggy-dog.

"Maybe so," she said, winking, "but you wouldn't be here if *you* didn't."

"Mitch didn't win the contest," Gary Conrad said. "Were you disappointed, kid?"

"Yes," I told him. "I wanted to win more than anything. My friend Willie Ruth Jennings of Murfreesboro, Tennessee, she won five thousand dollars." I smiled at the camera, sure she was watching. "She's a very good cook."

"And what would you have done with all that money, a kid twelve years old? Since you're a health food nut, you wouldn't have bought a ton of lollipops and jaw breakers, now, would you?" The audience laughed as he rolled his eyes. The camera with the red beam moved closer to me. This is the picture that would have shown them my lice, I thought, and I laughed, too.

"Well," I said, and I suddenly spotted Dad in the audience, "it would have come in handy, the money would." Dad grinned at me. "My parents' natural food store, Sunshine, burned down the day before I left for the contest. It was destroyed." The audience gasped. Gary Conrad put down the pencil he was doodling with.

"The whole place was destroyed?" Walt Milliken asked.

"Yes," I told him, and suddenly, looking again at Dad, I saw he wasn't grinning anymore. It was like the wind changed, and the air was suddenly cold. Tears swooshed up in my eyes. There wasn't anything I could do about it. I didn't want to talk about the fire any more. I didn't want to entertain people with it. I didn't want to talk about how it looked or smelled.

"My mom went out today looking for another job," I said fast, blinking my eyes, "and my dad and me were talking on the plane coming out here about maybe opening a place, a small place nearer our house, and near the university, between a camp fitter's store and a book store. We'd sell takeout. It'd be a natural food deli." One of the tears escaped and rolled down my cheek. I rubbed it away with my hand. "We'd call it Sunshine to Go. Dad says we could use some of my recipes. We'd have fresh fruit cups; veggies vinaigrette; avocado, cheese, and sprouts in pita bread; cucumber salad; you know. Sometimes we'd have my gingerbread. And for sure, we'd serve Banana Tofu Milkshake, like the kind I'm going to make tonight."

"Well, let's see if we go-fu that," Gary Conrad said cheerfully. He stood up, looking pleased I wasn't going to bawl all over the stage. "Can I help?"

"Sure," I told him. He led me over to the place where all the cooking stuff I'd brought along was set up. The table was in the same spot they'd been playing basketball a few minutes before. He opened up a drawer, pulled out a floppy white chef's cap, and plopped it on my head. The audience laughed. I scrubbed my hands with a warm wet towel on the table, and gave it to Gary Conrad. "I feel like a surgeon," he said.

He sliced the three frozen peeled bananas while I put the rest of the ingredients into the blender I'd brought all the way from home.

"Tofu is soft soybean curd," I told everybody as I crumbled it into the blender, "very rich in protein. I use six ounces of it with three frozen bananas. You can put it in salads, salad dressing, curry dip, lots of things." I dropped the bananas into the blender, added a tablespoon of honey, two tablespoons of peanut butter, a pinch of nutmeg, and a quarter cup of cold milk. "You want to turn it on?" I asked him.

With a flourish Gary Conrad turned the switch, and we watched the milkshake twirl until it was smooth.

I poured him a paper-cupful. He downed it and smiled. There was a milkshake moustache on his lip. "Your Sunshine is going to go a long way, kid," he said to me.

To the camera he said, "And now hear this." It was commercial time.

Walt Milliken took a paper cup of my milkshake. Dawn said no thank you. Just before they went on the air again, Gloria swooped on the stage and off we went through the green curtains. On the other side, the zoo person stood, a box in one hand, a big, bright red-and-green parrot on her shoulder. I reached up and took off the chef's cap.

"No kidding, you're great, Gary," Alexandra said.

"Thank you," I told her, thinking she'd forgotten my name.

"No kidding, you're great, Gary," she said again.

"No kidding, you're great, Gary," the bird on her shoulder answered.

"No kidding, you're great, Gary," she said.

"No kidding, you're great, Gary, *awrkkkkkkk.*"

"Good bird."

"Good bird, *awrkkkkk.*"

Gloria opened the curtains and in they went to the heat, the red eye, and the Los Angeles skyline. I wasn't jealous at all.

In the cool, air-conditioned greenroom, I tossed the white cap on a table, sat back in a big leather chair, and tried to make my hands stop shaking. The TV monitor was still turned up loud.

"What do you have to say to Gary, Sherlock?" Alexandra was asking the bird.

Nothing. The bird lifted up his leg and pecked at his feathers.

"No kidding, you're great, Gary," she said to the bird.

Nothing. The bird turned his head from side to side, dumb.

I turned the sound down and closed my eyes.

Gloria stuck her head in the door. "Phone for you, Mitch. It's your public out there. Take it on the phone in the corner. Just push down the button that says 6230."

While I couldn't imagine who could be calling, I pushed 6230.

"Hello."

"Mitch?"

"Mom. How are you? How was it?"

"Mitch, you were wonderful. I was so proud. Is it warm there? It snowed here again after you left."

"Yes, it's warm. It's OK."

"Where did the idea for a natural food deli come from?" she asked.

"I don't know. It's just an idea. I kept trying to get Dad to say he'd open Sunshine again. And he kept saying he wasn't so sure. And then I remembered Mr. Corso and how much takeout he sells. And you know they do eat more health food over near the university. Dad and I would do it ourselves. You think it would work?"

"It's worth talking about, if you're sure you realize that I'm not . . . Is your dad there?"

"No, not yet. The show's not over and he's in the audience. You want to talk to him?"

"No. Yes. Oh, Mitch, I've got something terrible to tell you both." I got a sharp pain in my stomach. "It's about Sunshine. I found out today why it burned. The fire marshal's office called. They said they thought I'd want to know. . . ."

"Was it arson?"

"Arson? Oh, no. At least, not exactly."

"Not exactly? What's that supposed to mean?"

The line clicked and I was afraid we were cut off. "Mom?"

"They told me that from the intensity of the fire around an electrical outlet they'd decided it started there." I could hear her take a breath. "And that inside they found some remains of—" *click* "—ice."

"Ice? Lice? Was it lice?"

"Mice," she said. "Mice. Don't you see what that means? It was mice chewing on wires inside the outlet box that started the fire. At least that's what the official report said. Do you see what that means?"

"It means that mice started the fire."

"It means, Mitch, that *I* started the fire. I wouldn't let the exterminators in. I *had* seen a mouse or two, but I didn't want to poison them. My traps didn't seem to do it. Maybe I should have emptied the whole store and let the exterminators in. But the poison would still have been there. I *couldn't* let them do it."

"You didn't have anything to do with the fire, Mom. That's crazy," I told her. "You aren't a mouse."

"Mitch, listen. I was tired of running the store and wanted to get rid of it. I didn't let the exterminators kill the mice. The mice burned the store. Therefore, *I* burned the store."

"Mom, if I talked like that you'd ask me where I'd been eating root-beer popsicles and marshmallows."

There was another click on the line.

"Mitch," she said, "this is costing us a mint. Have your dad call me, will you? And you *were* great, no kidding."

"That's what the parrot was supposed to say to Gary Conrad," I told her. " 'No kidding, you're great, Gary.' Did he ever say it?"

"No," she said, laughing, "but he did swear so long and loud they had to take him away. I was only listening in case they said something else about you, but there are some things you can't help hearing."

Gloria came in the greenroom carrying a wooden box. Inside the box, the parrot was saying, "*Awrrrrrk*, good bird, no kidding." Gloria looked like she'd had a hard day. "Good bird, no kidding," she said, and stuck the box in a corner.

"Mitch, you've got another call holding," she whispered. "There's a click on the line to tell you that one's waiting. It's on 6231, I think."

"Mom," I said, "forget the mice. Please." Somehow I had to cheer her up. "Did you read your horoscope today?" *Click*, went the phone.

"No," she said. "I read the want ads instead. Even called a few ad agencies. Some seem possible."

"I read your horoscope on the plane and saved it for you," I told her. And then I made one up. "Do what you think is best. Everything will be all right. Express happiness."

Click, went the phone.

"Mitch," she said, "you're OK. Forget about asking your father to call. I'll talk to you both when you get home." And she hung up.

Button 6231 was flashing red on the phone. I pressed it and said hello.

"Mitch?" a voice said.

"Yes?" I couldn't imagine who besides Mom would be calling.

"It's me."

"Me?"

"It's me, Willie Ruth. You were darling. You really were. I loved it when you mentioned my name. I loved it, even if it was mean of you to say I'm a good cook."

"Hi, Willie Ruth. At least I didn't say you'd been cooking since you were an *infant*."

"Mitch, you know that five thousand dollars I won? Daddy says I should buy a colt with it."

"A colt?" I tried not to think of all the things we could have bought for five thousand dollars—a new peanut butter maker, a blinking yellow neon sign that said "Sunshine to Go," a machine that makes soft frozen honey yogurt. Maybe we should advertise on WOGR, I thought, and Leroi Rupert would do something great for us.

"Mitch? Mitch?" she went on. "He's going to be my eleventh horse, but he's the first one I'll buy with my very own money and I get to train him. Mamma said I should name him Toad in the Hole, but I think that's a hateful name, don't you? Daddy said I could name him whatever I wanted. . . . Oh, and Mitch," she said, "I lost your Cubs cap in the airport. Could you send me another one to remember you by?"

The program was over and everybody was coming into the greenroom laughing about the parrot.

"Sure," I told her. "A red one or a blue one?"

"Doesn't matter. Just so it's yours. Oh, Mitch, the craziest thing happened. You're not going to believe it. Mamma was like to died. When I got home Mamma discovered that . . . you promise not to tell, now . . ."

"I promise," I said, watching Dawn Couture hug everybody goodbye.

"What happened was, my head was itching like crazy and Mamma discovered that I had *lice*. She like to died. She said nice girls don't get lice. So, anyway, I got my hair cut short today and got this special shampoo. Mamma said it was the airplane headrest that I got them from."

"Willie Ruth . . ." I said, but I didn't have the heart to tell her.

"Yes?"

"Thanks for calling."

"I'm glad you were on the show instead of me. I mean it. I didn't really have all that much to say."

"I've gotta go," I told her. I wanted to get Walt Milliken's autograph before he left. And Dawn Couture was coming over to give me a hug. I didn't want to miss it.

"Mitch," she said, "you know what I'm going to name my new colt?"

"No," I told her. "Tell me."

"I'm going to name it," she said, "My Gingerbread Man."

"Willie Ruth," I gulped, "you are too much."

"I know," she said. "It'll be a real show horse, too. A winner. Next time you're in Tennessee you drop by, now."

"Good bird," the parrot shrieked from its box.

"I will, Willie Ruth. I sure will." I hung up the phone. Dawn Couture gave me a big, perfumed, pink-feathery hug. I could hardly wait to tell Aaron and Lenny. In the doorway Dad stood with his arms folded, grinning at me. I beamed back as the feathers tickled my nose.

"OK, Sunshine," Dad said, "it's time for us to go."

ABOUT THE AUTHOR

'I know why you write about us,' a sixth-grade boy once told me. 'It's because we're middle-aged and things are happening to us.' And it's true. My characters are all in the process of growing up, of being astonished by the strange way their world works.

"You can see yourself and your weaknesses in someone else as easily when you are laughing at his muddle as when you are weeping at his despair. That's what I try to do—make my readers laugh and understand at the same time.

"Before writing I always do research. I've talked to boys about collecting beer cans, to refugees about what it was like coming to America, to teachers of children with learning disabilities. I once went with a class to outdoor education camp. I've asked kids what it was like to be in programs for the gifted and talented. It is this close observation that I hope makes my books seem real."

Born in Beardstown, Illinois, Jamie Gilson spent her early years in several small midwestern towns where her father worked as a flour miller. After graduating from Northwestern University, she married Jerome Gilson, then a law student and now a trademark lawyer. In addition to writing, Mrs. Gilson has worked as a junior high school speech and English teacher; a staff writer and producer for the Division of Radio and Television of the Chicago Public Schools; and as continuity director for radio station WFMT. The Gilsons have three grown children, Tom, Matthew, and Anne, and live in a suburb of Chicago.